Mila the Magician
《魔劫》

Zhang Jian
章簡

Proverse Hong Kong
文韻

Mila the Magician
By Zhang Jian
章簡
2nd bilingual edition published in Hong Kong
by Proverse Hong Kong,
August 2016
Copyright © Proverse Hong Kong, November 2016.
ISBN: 978-988-8228-62-1
Available from: https://www.createspace.com/6412770

Bilingual edition 1st published in Hong Kong
by Proverse Hong Kong, January 2014.
Copyright © Proverse Hong Kong, January 2014.
ISBN 978-988-8227-01-3

Enquiries: Proverse Hong Kong, P. O. Box 259, Tung Chung Post Office, Tung Chung,
Lantau Island, NT, Hong Kong SAR, China.
E-mail: proverse@netvigator.com
Web site: www.proversepublishing.com

The right of Zhang Jian 章簡
to be identified as the author of this work has been asserted by her in accordance with
the Copyright, Designs and Patents Act 1988.

Bilingual lay-out by Tony M. T. Yip 葉明德.
Cover design, Proverse Hong Kong and Artist Hong Kong Company.
Illustrations and cover image by Cheng Yee-Ying 鄭綺盈.

British Library Cataloguing in Publication Data. A catalogue record for the
first bilingual edition of this book is available
from the British Library.

《魔劫》
章簡

中英文雙語版第二版於二零一六年八月
由文韻於香港出版
2016 年 11 月版權所有©文韻
國際書號 ISBN 978-988-8228-62-1
可於https://www.createspace.com/6412770瀏覽

中英文雙語版第一版於二零一四年一月
由文韻出版
2014 年 1 月版權所有©文韻
國際書號 ISBN 978-988-8227-01-3

查詢：文韻
地址：中國香港特別行政區新界大嶼山東涌郵政局郵政信箱 259 號
電子郵件：proverse@netvigator.com
網址：www.proversepublishing.com

章簡（Zhang Jian）女士之權利
按照英國 1988 年《版權、外觀設計和專利法》，
章簡（Zhang Jian）女士宣稱其為本作品之原作者

中英文雙語版由葉明德（Tony M. T. Yip）先生負責設計排版
封面設計由文韻及香港印藝負責
插圖及封面圖片由鄭綺盈（Cheng Yee-Ying）女士負責

英國倫敦大英圖書館編目資料
本書之編目紀錄可見於英國倫敦大英圖書館

To the Reader

MILA THE MAGICIAN tells the adventures of a young man, Mila, who leaves home to learn black magic. After overcoming many difficulties, he becomes a powerful sorcerer.

An adventure story; it is also a tale of revenge, as it delves into the psychology and ramifications of vengeance.

Mila is motivated by the desire to take revenge against his evil uncle and aunt, who have robbed him of his inheritance and left his mother and sister destitute. But successful revenge does not make Mila happy. He is deeply remorseful as he has harmed many innocent people. In penitence, he turns to Buddhism, and eventually he becomes a great saint.

This tale of magic is not completely imaginary; it follows the traditional beliefs and folklore of Tibet. The narration has a Buddhist perspective; loosely based on the early life of the great Tibetan saint Milarepa (11th C. AD).

It is not a biography; but an entertaining story set in Tibet, with its beautiful scenery and rich culture.

Acknowledgements

Grateful thanks to the Editors:
Tony M. T. Yip 葉明德 (Chinese text)
Proverse Hong Kong with Robin Louise Pile (English text)

致讀者

《魔劫》可說是有娛樂性的青年歷險故事。米拉離家去尋師學魔法。他經歷過許多劫難，又克服了無數的障礙，終於成功為大法師。但如果把《魔劫》當作復仇故事，就會更有意義。其中有關於復仇心態的描述，以及復仇的種種後果。

米拉學巫術的動機是為了要向他邪惡的叔父及姑母報復。他們搶奪了他家的全部財產，令米拉的母親和妹妹無以為生。結果他大仇得報，但他並不開心，他反而深深懺悔，因為他用巫術傷害了很多無辜的人。

故事中有關魔幻的描述，作者沿用了西藏的民間習俗和傳說。顯然蘊藏着佛教精神和思維，因為故事的源頭就是西藏、米拉日巴大師青年時的事蹟。作者並非寫他的傳記，作者的目標是一個有娛樂性的故事，背景是西藏的大自然美景和豐富的民族風情。

特別鳴謝

謹此向以下諸位致意，鳴謝其編輯服務：
葉明德（Tony M. T. Yip）（中文版）
文韻、Robin Louise Pile（英文版）

ADVANCE RESPONSE TO 'MILA THE MAGICIAN'
Impressions of My Reading

This is a good story told in magnificent prose, interposed with poetry, and the result is exquisite. Evidently, the author has talent, wit, even genius. She has made good use of her own life experience, writing fluently and vividly, to create this very special novel. In a humane way, she makes a thorough inquiry, probing and leading us into a realm of mystery and religious complexes. The reader's curiosity is immediately aroused and his attention engaged. The total effect shows that the author has fulfilled her design. Everyone should take notice, for this book has value.

LOMEN
12 December 2012

讀後的感言　羅門

這是以瑰麗的詩文、散文所渾和與轉化成的一本溢流故事性的精美小說；由於作者有可見的才情才思才智與體驗及其生動通暢流利的文筆，便能得心應手的將這本特殊小說，導入充滿人性化及有探索探究探幽與宗教情結的神秘之境，大大的吸引住讀者閱讀的好奇心與興趣、進入其境，而臻至預期的意願與表現效果，值得大家珍視與關注。

2012 年 12 月 12 日

Preface

Many people think of Tibet as a difficult place to visit because of its steep terrain, severe cold weather and its inaccessibility. Tibet is even more mysterious to the outside world because of its way of life: not only is it theocratic, but its esoteric beliefs date back in history, involving the so called "Tantric Buddhism", "Black Sect" and sorcery. In the 5th Century B.C., Bonn was the religion for the whole of Tibet: worshipping the sun, moon, mountains, rivers, cattle, sheep and wild animals. A thousand years later, Buddhism came from India and competed with Bonn. The two religions kept their differences but also learnt from each other, and gradually became assimilated. There are still a million worshippers of Bonn to-date.

In this bilingual story by Ms. Luo Zhang-lan, the protagonist Milarepa is a household name, a great Tibetan Buddhist. The narration is all about his struggles before he is converted to Buddhism. In the book, his name is Mila (Mila Thopaga). The author chooses to portray his early life, as a youth who wants to learn black magic and goes through adventures to find a teacher. She is not wholly constrained by the facts of biography, and she does not emphasize the supernatural prowess of the great lama. She only cares to describe how he overcomes impossible odds. The biggest revelation in the book is this: because of the destruction of his family, Mila is angry and deliberately learns sorcery for the purpose of revenge. However, his revenge also harms innocent villagers. He finally realizes his sin in practicing sorcery.

Milarepa was not only a great ascetic lama, a paradigm of Buddhism, he was also a poet. The author cites as many as eleven excerpts of Milarepa's poetry, to build up a poetic effect. This bilingual book is fascinating. The English writing is fluent and readable. The Chinese writing is somewhat westernized, but

《魔劫》先睹誌感　余光中

西藏地勢高峻、氣候嚴寒、交通不便，外人視為畏途。但更令外人感到神秘的，是藏族的生活方式，不僅以僧侶立國，而且宗教信仰源遠流長，並涉及所謂「密宗」、「黑教」、「魔法」。公元前五世紀，西藏全境奉行的是苯教，崇拜的對象是日月山水、牛羊野獸。一千多年後佛教自印度傳入，兩教相競的結果互有迎拒，漸漸交融。苯教信徒仍有近百萬人。

羅章蘭女士這本英漢對照的故事，以藏傳佛教深入民心的大師米拉日巴為主角，所述種種都是他皈依佛教以前的掙扎。在書中他的名字叫米拉（米拉特巴加）。羅章蘭有意把他的前半生寫成一位冒險尋師苦習魔法的青年，並不完全拘泥事實。她無意誇張高僧的超人奇蹟，只在意他如何終於修煉到最高的境界。書中最大的啟示，該是米拉憤於家庭被毀，刻意習得魔咒以為報復，然而復仇之餘竟害到無辜村民，終於覺悟使行魔法已造惡業。

米拉日巴不僅是苦行高僧、佛法典範，也是詩人。所以羅章蘭在書中引証其詩達十一段之多，以助詩情。這本書漢英對照，引人入勝，英文寫得流暢可讀，中文略顯西化，卻

straight-forward and pleasant. The author won a prize for translation from English to Chinese (the "Leung Shi Qiu Literary Prize") some years ago. No wonder she can use both English and Chinese in "Mila the Magician" – a two-pronged attack – to write this interesting book! I am happy to write this preface to recommend it.

Professor YU Kuang Chung
Kaohsiung, Taiwan
9th March 2013

寫得平易近人，樸實可親。羅章蘭多年前曾獲「梁實秋文學獎」的英譯中獎項，難怪她這次能中英雙管齊下，寫出一本有趣的書，故樂於作序推薦。

余光中
2013.3.9
台灣高雄

Author's Introduction

The story is about the adventures of young Mila, who has taken on the impossible mission of learning Black Magic to destroy his family's enemies. It is not completely imaginary but is based on the life of a historical figure. Mila is drawn from the legend of Milarepa, the great Tibetan guru. Milarepa (1066-1135) is said to have achieved enlightenment and become Buddha in his lifetime. He has been an inspiration for the Tibetan people throughout the ages. Single-minded in his pursuit of religion, he overcame all obstacles and triumphed against impossible odds to become a superman.

A more true to life history of Milarepa's is by his disciple Rechung, who claims to have recorded Milarepa's own words. Milarepa is known to have possessed extraordinary powers: to fly, to go without food for months, to show up in many places at the same time, to appear physically as a snow leopard.

Great yogis develop their magical abilities through mind control, although such abilities are incidental and not the real aim of their spiritual pursuits. Scientists have observed and studied some phenomena of self control such as: the deliberate alteration of the pulse rate, even stopping of the heart beat, the arrest of a hemorrhage after a deep cut and the subsequent quick healing. A similar known phenomenon is suspended animation,

前言

這是一個青年人的歷險故事。米拉離開家鄉去尋師學黑魔法。因為他的媽媽命令米拉學會黑魔法來為她復仇。目標是要毀滅他的伯父和姑母，他們強奪了米拉的全部家產，使米拉一家人無以為生。這故事並非全屬虛構，而是改編自西藏佛教米拉日巴大師（1066—1135）的生平事蹟。米拉日巴大師是西藏佛教噶舉派（白教）的始祖瑪爾巴大師的弟子。藏人相信米拉日巴大師以他一生的功業，在世成佛。

這故事只是描述一個青年人尋求魔法，並不根據史實。流傳下來的米拉日巴大師傳記是由他的大弟子岡波巴撰寫，其中包括有米拉日巴大師生平的語錄。傳說中米拉日巴大師非常神奇，他實踐的奇蹟包括：肉身飛行，絕食數月之久，化身成為雪豹，在不同的地點同時現身。這些不可思議的事跡可說是藏人信仰的一部分。

有極高修為的瑜珈師是能夠實踐奇蹟的，雖然這並非他們修行的最終目標，而是他們到達了最高境界的一種現象。科學家亦有實地去研究一些奇蹟，例如：瑜珈大師能刻意改變脈率，甚至使心臟停止跳動一分鐘。能使自己身體的創傷

akin to animal hibernation. It is said that yogis have been buried alive and remained unharmed when dug up again several weeks later. When an expert asks a great guru to display such powers for his benefit, the guru will deny that he has any. A great guru only uses his powers for the instruction and benefit of his disciples, as Milarepa did for his followers just before he died.

As directed by his guru Marpa, Milarepa practiced "Tum-mo", the development of vital heat. It is well known in Tibet that Yogis can sit naked on snow and perspire freely so that the snow around them melts. Milarepa lived as a hermit in the caves of the snowy Himalayan Mountains, clothed only in a thin cotton garment. The people named him Milarepa, meaning "Mila, the Cotton Clad". His real name was Mila Thopaga, as given by his father when he was born, meaning "Delightful to hear". Born in a wealthy family, Thopaga's father died when he was seven. The family's fortune was taken over by his evil uncle and aunt. Young Mila, together with his mother and sister, had to endure the hardship of field labour and suffered insults from their neighbours. He was commanded by his mother to learn black magic so that he could take revenge on his uncle and aunt.

This story is about young Mila in search of black magic, wandering from place to place, from teacher to teacher. Overcoming insurmountable obstacles, he acquired the powers of a sorcerer. Then he used black magic to destroy his enemies,

極速恢復及立即止血。比較易見到的奇蹟就是生機暫停，如動物冬眠。曾有瑜珈大師被活埋數周，被挖掘出來仍然無恙。每當科學家要求這些大師行奇蹟來驗證時，他們都否認自己有行奇蹟的超能力。大師們只會利用神跡來傳授弟子。米拉日巴大師在快要離世時，也曾向弟子們顯示連串的神跡。

米拉日巴得到瑪爾巴大師的傳授，能夠控制自己的體溫。不少藏人都見過的神奇現象就是：一個瑜珈大師赤身流汗的坐在雪地上，他周圍的雪在溶化。米拉日巴隱居在喜瑪拉雅山的雪洞中，他只穿着棉布單衣，所以人們稱他為米拉日巴（穿棉布單衣的米拉）。他的原名是米拉特巴加，是他父親給他起的名字（悅耳聲的意思）。

米拉日巴在七歲時父親過世，家產全部被伯父和姑母奪去。米拉和媽媽、妹妹要過非常窮困的生活，在田裏做農工，又被村人欺負。媽媽命令米拉去學黑魔法來報復他們被奪家產的仇恨。

這故事描述青年米拉冒險尋師學魔法的過程。最後他成功了！利用黑魔法誅殺了伯父及親屬、鄰里，又降雹盡毀了

his aunt and uncle. However, as he had grown spiritually, successful vengeance did not bring him joy or satisfaction. He now felt the ashen taste of revenge. When he saw the havoc that he had wrought, including the destruction of life, he became deeply remorseful. He repented of his sins and went forth to seek true religion.

True to his name, "Thopaga", Milarepa had a beautiful singing voice. He was also gifted with poetry and expressed his innermost thoughts in his famous "The Hundred Thousand Songs". Actually, the number of his known poems is only about two hundred and fifty. Chanted by traveling singers, the poems have been a source of learning and delight to all Tibetans. Common people who do not study in monasteries can absorb their religion and culture through oral tradition.

Milarepa was a mystic and did not write purely for aesthetic pleasure, although sometimes he wrote beautifully about nature. His songs are primarily didactic, teaching the basic tenets of Buddhism, or expressing his own religious experience and insight. To give some idea of the Tibetan oral tradition, I have incorporated some "chants" or poems in the story. These poems are drawn mainly from "The Hundred Thousand Songs", but I have transposed them freely. To my best ability, I have paid tribute to the greatness of Tibetan culture and to the beauty of the land.

家鄉的莊稼。當他眼見被他毀壞的一切，他感到罪過又深深的懺悔了。後來他再次出發，去尋訪老師學佛以求解脫，經過多年艱苦的修行，終於得成正果。

米拉有歌唱的天賦，好嗓子，正如他的原名特巴加（悅耳聲）。他又有詩才，所以慣常以詩歌來表達他的內心。米拉日巴的十萬歌頌是最珍貴的西藏文學遺產。其實他流傳下來的詩歌大約是二百五十多篇。他弘法傳道的方式是採用了西藏民間的詩歌唱誦式。雖然他的目標是說教，但他對大自然的描述極賦美感。我把一些源自米拉日巴的詩句，彙編進我的故事中，來形容西藏民間的口述傳統。我寫這故事的目標是為了讚頌西藏地域之美，及向偉大的西藏文化致敬！

MILA THE MAGICIAN: TABLE OF CONTENTS

ILLUSTRATIONS

《魔劫》 目錄

插圖

Mila Thopaga

米拉特巴加

Chapter 1
THE MILA FAMILY

The village of Kyanga Tsai sat on a small plateau, at the junction of two rivers that carved through the Himalayas, flowing into Nepal. Isolated in a land of snowy peaks and glistering glaciers, Kyanga Tsai could only be reached by crossing ravines and bridges. In autumn, the village seemed submerged in a sea of golden barley. At the centre, a large red monastery crowned the golden fields, its gleaming gold roof and filligreed towers like a fairy palace. The compound occupied the summit of a hill, and was encircled by a rampart twenty feet high. Of the hundred mud-brick houses clustered around the monastery, one house, standing a little apart in a large lot, was noticeably taller and larger than the rest. It was the best house in the village, known as the "Four And Eight", for its three stories rested on four decorated columns and eight poplar pillars. This was the house where Mila Thopaga was born.

On approaching, it appeared rather dilapidated and seemed deserted. A few chickens pecked the ground in the courtyard, but the large stable under the house was completely empty of animals. Entrance to the living areas upstairs was achieved by climbing a ladder from the courtyard. The large living room was clean and orderly, although the floral paintings on the walls had

第一章
米拉氏家族

古老的<u>貢唐村</u>坐落在小高原上，山下繞着兩條交匯的河流，奔向<u>尼泊爾</u>。這村莊獨處雪山峰頂，周圍是熠熠生輝的冰河，對外交通全靠一條狹窄的山路，宛延穿過峽谷，跨過橋樑。秋天，這村莊就像淹沒在金黃色的麥穗海洋裏。村子中央有一座宏偉的廟宇，就像金色田野的皇冠，其閃爍的金頂和精緻的尖塔宛如仙宮。廟院圍着二十呎高的牆佔據了整個山頂。廟外擠着數百間土磚搭建的民居。其中最高大的一間較為獨立，明顯是這裏最好的房屋，三層樓高，有四根精心雕飾的大圓柱和八根白楊木的大樑，大家稱它為「四柱八樑」。<u>米拉</u>就出生在這裏。

近看又發覺它很破舊，好像被荒廢了。庭院裏有幾隻小雞在地上啄食，而房屋下層的牲口棚卻是空蕩蕩的，要到樓上的居所，就要從院子裏的樓梯爬上去。那大客廳收拾得乾淨又整齊，儘管在牆上的畫已褪色，本來精緻的雕花窗框亦殘破不堪。但這房間一點也不荒涼！地板上鋪着五顏六色的

faded and the intricately carved window frames were chipped. However, at this particular time, it was far from deserted! Many colourful rugs were scattered on the floor, giving the room a festive air, and thick, stuffed mattresses for seating were arranged around low tables, for the room had been made ready for a large gathering.

All the present activities were found in the large ground-floor kitchen, separate from the house. Four women were busily preparing food for a feast. The kitchen was perfectly clean and the cooked meat and pastries sat in neat piles. White Garland bustled around, checking the food. Her real name was Karmo-ken, but the villagers had named her White Garland when she was a beautiful young girl. Now a widow in her late thirties, she was tall and slim, and moved nimbly with sparkling eyes, but her still-lovely face looked haggard. White Garland had been married to Mila Serab, who had died of illness eight years ago. She lived in this house with her two children, Mila Thopaga, her fifteen-year-old son, and Peta, her eleven-year-old daughter. Peta was helping in the kitchen while her brother had gone out on an errand. Urmo, a stout old woman in a dark green robe, bent over an open fire toasting *qinke* (highland barley) for *zanba* (the Tibetan staple food). She was the nursemaid who had brought up Mila and Peta.

Peta chatted and giggled with Zesay, a pretty fourteen

地氈，很多小矮桌周圍擺滿了厚厚的坐墊，整個房間的佈置帶有節日的氣氛，好像為迎接一場盛大的聚會，做了精心的準備。

所有的現場活動都集中在院子裏的一個獨立大廚房。這個廚房非常乾淨，烹調好的肉類和麵餅均擺放有序。白花冠正忙碌地檢查各種食物。她本來名叫娘切葛簡，在她還是一位年輕漂亮的小姑娘時，村民們就開始叫她白花冠。現在她已年近四十，是一位寡婦，又高又瘦，她靈敏地走來走去，眼睛裏充滿了活力，但她可愛的臉盤看上去還是有些憔悴。白花冠的丈夫叫誰熱嘉參，八年前不幸因病去世。她與自己的兩個孩子一起住在這所房子裏，她的兒子叫米拉特巴加，十五 歲，女兒叫百德，十一歲。百德正在廚房裏幫忙，她哥哥則出門辦事去了。奶娘是一位年邁的矮胖婦女，身穿一件深綠色的長袍，她彎腰在爐火上烤着用來製作酥油茶的青稞。她是一位保姆，米拉和百德都是她帶大的。

澤思很漂亮，十四歲，穿着一件繡花長袍，帶着松石的

year-old, who wore an embroidered robe and turquoise in her hair braids. The two girls sat at a low table, making buns out of wheat dough.

Nurse Urmo looked up and said to White Garland, "I'm so glad to be here! Just like the old days before Master passed away. Isn't it decent of Aunt Palden to let me come back for a few days to help out?"

White Garland disagreed, frowning. "Palden doesn't understand the word decent! She is rich now, since she has robbed us of our entire fortune, but she is forever hungry for a feast because she used to beg for food in her youth. She is never shy to take something more from us." She added, "To be fair, Palden isn't the only ungrateful one. Of all those who were frequent guests at our table, none seem to remember us now, except to sneer and to laugh at our misfortune!"

Nurse said to her comfortingly, "Don't worry, your troubles will soon be over. Now that Thopaga is fifteen years old and is of age, he can claim back his fortune. According to Mila Serab's will, Uncle Gyaltsen and his sister, Aunt Palden, must now release the property. Thopaga will marry Zesay and live here. Very soon, this house will be happy and prosperous once more!"

Peta giggled and said to Zesay, "No wonder you look like a bride!" Zesay blushed and lowered her head.

White Garland was not reassured. "Uncle and Aunt will

髮帶，她與百德在聊天，不時發出哈哈的笑聲。兩個小姑娘坐在矮桌旁，正在用小麥麵團做麵包。

奶娘抬頭對白花冠說：「我很高興能夠來到這裏！感覺像回到了老爺還在的時光。是不是白卓姑媽想得周到，讓我回來幫幾天忙的？」

白花冠不同意，反對道：「白卓才不是想得周到呢！她現在有錢了，因為她掠奪了我們的所有財富，但她總是渴望參加宴會，因為她年輕的時候曾經乞討過。」她又補充說：「當然，也不是只有白卓一個人不領情。原來我們家的所有常客，現在都想不起我們了，他們只會對我們家的不幸遭遇冷嘲熱諷！」

奶娘安慰她說：「別擔心，一切困難很快都會過去的。現在特巴加有十五歲了，已經長大成人了，他可以索回他的財富。依據他父親的遺囑，格列伯父和他的妹妹，也就是白卓姑媽現在必須歸還這些財產。特巴加會和澤思結婚並住在這裏。很快，這座房屋又會再次充滿幸福和繁榮的景象！」

百德笑着對澤思說：「你看上去就像一個新娘子！」澤思臉紅了，低下了頭。

這些話並沒有打消白花冠的疑慮，她說：「伯父和姑媽不會善甘休的。他們密謀策劃了這麼多年才得到我們的財

never give up without a fight. They schemed and plotted for years to get our property! They'll lie and cheat, and do everything they can to hang on to it. They are terrible fighters, and I am not so sure that we can win!"

"I was there in the room when Master made his last will just before he died," Nurse said. "Oh, I can remember every detail! He was so ill but he asked to be carried down to the living room. Fifty relatives and friends gathered around him. We all knew that he was dying. He made Uncle Gyaltsen and Aunt Palden guardians of his children and property, but he said clearly that Thopaga would inherit all that he left behind. He also said, 'I shall be watching you from the realm of the dead!' He died later that evening."

"You are right," White Garland said. "That's why he betrothed Thopaga to Zesay, so that when they married, they would manage the whole property. His will was put into writing and all those present were witnesses. For tomorrow's party, I have invited those fifty witnesses, and they must see to it that we are treated fairly."

"Oh Mother," Peta said, "we'll have good food and nice clothes and Zesay will be my sister-in-law. How happy we'll be!"

"You were the best family in the village," Nurse said. "The wealthiest and the best connected. Everyone in the village

產！他們一直在撒謊和欺騙大家，竭盡全力地把持着這些財產。他們簡直壞透了，我們可能鬥不過他們！」

「主人臨終前表達自己最後的遺願時我也在場，」奶娘說：「每個細節我都記得一清二楚！那時他非常虛弱，但他還是要求家人把自己抬到客廳。當時他周圍有五十位親朋好友。我們都知道他快不行了。他讓伯父格列和姑媽白卓照顧他的孩子和財產，但他明確地說過特巴加將繼承他留下的一切。他還說他會在天堂看着大家！那天深夜他就離開了人世。」

「你說得對，」白花冠說：「這就是他讓特巴加與澤思訂婚的原因，等他們結婚後，他們就可以掌管全部財產。他的遺願已經用書面形式確立下來，所有在場的人都是見證者。我已經邀請了這五十位見證者來參加明天的聚會，他們必須看到我們得到公平的對待。」

「行了，媽媽」，百德說：「我們現在吃穿不愁，澤思也將成為我的嫂子。我們會生活得很幸福的！」

「你們一向是整個村子裏最體面的人家，」保姆說：「不僅最有錢，而且家人的關係也最為融洽。村裏的每個人都很

29

looked up to you because you have royal blood. Peta is too young to remember that I used to braid her hair daily with gold and turquoise. I weep when I think of what your life has been for the past eight years, working in the fields in summer for Uncle, spinning and carding wool in winter for Aunt. They worked you so hard and gave you food only fit for dogs. No wonder you are all so thin and weak! Your hands and feet are badly blistered. Peta now has lice in her hair. Why did you give up everything so easily?"

White Garland threw up her hands. "What choice did I have? The morning after the funeral, Uncle and his sons, together with Aunt and their servants, burst into our house. They pushed me into a room and kept me there with the children while they ransacked the house. Uncle took all the male ornaments and clothing, and Aunt took all my precious jewelry and beautiful gowns, which she had envied for years. The household wares, the fields and the animals, they divided between them. We were told to go and live with each of them in turn. We have been miserable and poor, and yet no one in the village has ever spoken out for us."

"How about your own people?" Nurse asked. "They should have stood up and fought for you."

White Garland said, "Uncle has three grown sons, all fierce and strong. On my side, there is my only brother, Thangme, and

尊敬你，因為你有皇室的血統。<u>百德</u>不會記得以前我每天都用金飾和寶石給她弄頭髮。在過去的八年裏，夏天你為伯父在田間勞作，冬天為姑媽辛勤紡紗，每當我想起你所過的日子，都會忍不住掉下眼淚。他們如此拼命地使喚你，給你吃的只是餵狗一樣的食物。難怪你現在又瘦又弱！你的手和腳都起滿繭了。<u>百德</u>頭上現在都長滿了蝨子。你為什麼就輕易放棄了一切呢？」

<u>白花冠</u>攤開兩手，無可奈何地說：「我有什麼辦法？葬禮結束後的那天早上，伯父帶着自己的兒子們，連同姑媽和他們的僕人一起衝進我們的家。他們強行把我關進一間小屋裏，讓我和孩子們呆在那裏。當時，他們對整所房屋進行了洗劫。伯父拿走了所有男人用的東西和衣服，而姑媽則搶走了我所有的貴重珠寶和漂亮的禮服。多年來她一直都很妒忌我所擁有的一切。陶器、田地和動物都被他們兩家瓜分了。我們被迫輪流寄宿在他們家，一直過得非常痛苦和可憐，但村子裏沒有人為我們說一句正義的話。」

「你自己的人呢？」奶娘問道：「他們應當站出來為你們撐腰。」

<u>白花冠</u>說：「伯父的三個兒子已長大成人，他們都很厲害，也很強壯。而我這邊只有一個哥哥：<u>唐美</u>，他這個人不愛說話，也不愛惹事生非。我們根本就不是他們的對手。在

Zesay's father who is a quiet and peaceful man. We are not strong enough to fight them. Uncle had been our estate manager, and already had control of our fields, animals, and the warehouse, two years before my husband died."

"I can't understand why Master put his trust in Uncle and Aunt instead of you," Nurse said. "They were only cousins from his native village, yet your husband was so loving and generous to you. People used to say that White Garland had both beauty and ability: how well she managed her household and nourished her family." White Garland continued bitterly, "And now they say, 'Rich man, able wife! Soft wool, fine blanket!' And also 'See what happens when the head of the household is no longer with us!' The villagers are laughing behind our back." She became distraught, suddenly sat down and said, "Oh Nurse, when I saw him dying, I didn't want to live. I married him at sixteen; he was twenty. He had been my whole life. I could have died of shame and sorrow that day when I found out that he had no faith in me! I live now only for my children."

Nurse comforted her. "I noticed that Master had changed in his last few years. He angered easily and rowed with you, which never happened previously, and he became unpredictable. He even dismissed Losang, who had been estate manager for years, and put Uncle in charge. That was very strange."

"He had heard a terrible rumor that Losang was my lover.

我丈夫去世前兩年，伯父就接管了我們的財產，我們的田地和動物以及倉庫都由他來掌控。」

「我不理解主人為什麼信任伯父和姑媽，而不是你，」奶娘說：「他們只不過是他本村的堂兄妹，你丈夫向來很愛你，對你也很慷慨。人們常說白花冠不僅漂亮，而且很能幹：她把自己的家裏管理得井井有條，而且家人的關係也不錯。」

「現在他們都在說：『男人富有、女人能幹！軟毛才能做出精細的毯子』他們還說，『看看一家之長不在的時候會是怎樣的情形！』村民們常常在背後嘲笑我們。」她情緒變得有些激動，突然坐了下來說：「唉！當我看到他快不行的時候，我也不想活了。我十六歲就嫁給了他，那時他二十歲。他一直是我生活的全部，當我發現他對我一點信心都沒有的時候，我的心就因羞愧和悲痛而死去！我現在活着完全是為了我的孩子們。」

奶娘安慰她說：「我注意到主人在去世前的幾年裏有些變化。他動不動就生氣並與你爭吵，這在以前從來沒有過，他變得越來越不可捉摸。他甚至還辭退了多年來的管家盧生，讓伯父來接管財產，讓人感到很費解。」

「他聽到一個可怕的謠言，說盧生是我的情人。他怎麼

How could he have believed that? Losang had been so loyal to him and had helped him to build up his fortune. How could he have suspected me, the mother of his children?" She sighed heavily. "When Thopaga was born, Losang rode hundreds of miles to North Mountains to give the news to Serab, who was so delighted that he immediately named his son Tho-pa-ga (Delightful-to-hear). We three had been such good friends all along. Suddenly, Serab's attitude changed entirely; he became angry and suspicious without cause! At least Losang was suitably rewarded and wasn't sent away empty handed. My husband was a generous man, but he treated his wife and children meaner than anyone."

Nurse coughed. "Actually, Aunt Palden started that vicious rumour. I heard her gossiping to the villagers many times. I had never mentioned it to you because I was afraid of causing trouble."

"I always knew that Palden was full of trickery," White Garland said angrily. "She schemed and plotted for years to get her hands on our money, and she finally succeeded. My heart is broken because my husband never trusted me, even when we were first married. My Nyang family descended from royalty, and he thought that we were too far above him. Oh husband, see how low we have fallen!"

Nurse said, "What do you mean? I don't quite understand."

34

能相信這個？盧生一直都對他那麼忠誠，幫助他積累財富。他怎麼能懷疑我，我可是他孩子的媽啊？」她深深地歎了口氣：「特巴加出生時，盧生騎馬跑到數百公里之外的北山將這個喜訊告訴誰熱，他得知後欣喜若狂，立即給兒子起名叫特巴加（意思是「聽到後很高興」）。我們三個人一直都是很不錯的朋友。突然之間，誰熱的態度完全轉變了，他總是無緣無故地發脾氣，變得疑心重重！至少盧生得到了應有的報酬，沒有空手離開。我的丈夫很慷慨，但他對自己的妻子和孩子比對任何人都吝嗇。」

奶娘咳嗽了一聲，說：「實際上，這個惡意的謠言是從姑媽白卓嘴裏傳出來的。我聽到她多次與村民們提起這事。我從來沒有跟你說過，因為我怕惹麻煩。」

「我一直都認為白卓很會欺騙人，」白花冠憤怒地說：「她多年來一直陰謀策劃想掠奪我們的金錢，最終她還是得逞了。我傷透了心，因為我的丈夫從來沒有信任過我，即便我們剛結婚時也是如此。我的南氏家族有皇室血統，他認為我們高高在上。唉！我的丈夫啊！現在你看看我們的地位有多低啊！」

奶娘說：「你說什麼？我不太明白。」

"When Uncle Gyaltsen and his sister Aunt Palden turned up unexpectedly from Chungwachi, like paupers, my father-in-law, Dorje, welcomed them with open arms. Amazingly, despite not being a generous man, he did everything to help them to settle into our village, even gave them money to start a business. Serab told me that he and his father were very glad to have their own relatives living nearby, for they felt overpowered by my family."

Nurse shook her head. "Uncle and Aunt are now so arrogant."

"Remember how humble they were," White Garland cried. "How they bowed and flattered! That's why Serab chose to entrust his property to his own tribe, rather than to his wife, mother of his children."

"He was very unwise," Nurse said. "And I must say that he wasn't good enough for you."

White Garland burst into tears. "Don't ever say that! He was my whole life."

"Things will get better," Nurse said, trying to soothe her. "You must look to the future for your children's sake."

Still feeling unsettled, White Garland rose and wandered from task to task, crooning a song to herself:

I am thinking of my husband, Serab,
Even though my hurt is great,
I still have the heart-felt wish to see you!
The more I suffer, the more I think of my husband,

「當伯父格列和他的妹妹白卓姑媽突然像乞丐一樣從松華芝來到我們面前時，我的公公多吉非常熱情地迎接了他們。令人吃驚的是，儘管他並不是一個很慷慨的人，但他卻想盡了一切辦法幫助他們安頓在我們村子裏，甚至還給他們錢讓他們在這裏創業。誰熱跟我說他和他父親對自己的親戚能住在附近感到非常高興，因為他們覺得太受制於我的家庭。」

奶娘搖了搖頭說：「伯父和姑媽現在太傲慢了。」

「想想以前他們是多麼地謙卑，」白花冠哭着說：「他們是如何對我們點頭哈腰、阿諛奉承的！這就是誰熱為什麼選擇將他的財產委託給他自己的部族，而不是給他的妻子，即他孩子的母親。」

「他太輕率了，」奶娘說：「我不得不說他對你不夠好。」

白花冠突然大哭了起來，說：「不要那麼說！他是我生活的全部。」

「情況會好起來的，」奶娘試圖安慰她說：「為了你的孩子，你必須向前看。」

白花冠仍覺得未佈置妥當，起身在各項工序間來回走動，嘴裏低聲地哼唱着：

我思念着我的丈夫誰熱，
儘管我受到了很大的傷害，
我還是滿懷熱情想見到你！
我受的苦越多，就越發思念我的丈夫，

At the time when I was with you, I was happy!
I am thinking of my husband,
Only you can relieve my suffering!

I am thinking of my father,
I think of my mother, more to me than a mother!
At the time living with them, I was happy.
Even though the distance is great,
Even though to find the way through darkness is
impossible,
My heart desires to see them!

On the top-floor of our dwelling, from the highest window,
You can see white clouds sail by.
On the seat for him, is the softest fleece of a lamb.
If my husband is sitting there, I'd be happy!
The more I suffer, the more I long to see him!
Even though my understanding is little,
Still my heart desires to see him
I think, I think of my dear husband,
The more I suffer, the more I think of him!

曾經與你在一起的日子，我感到非常幸福！
我思念着我的丈夫，
只有你才能減輕我的痛苦！

我思念着我的父親，
我也想念我的母親，她給我的一切遠遠超過了母親應給予的！
與他們生活在一起的日子，我曾經非常快樂；
儘管距離很遠，
儘管在黑暗中找不到路，
我渴望見到他們！

透過房屋頂層最高的那個窗戶，
你可以看到白雲飄過。
那是他的坐墊，用小羊身上最軟的毛編的。
如果我的丈夫端坐在那裏，我會感到非常開心！
我受的苦越多，就越想見到他！
儘管我不能理解，
我還是渴望見到他，
我無時無刻不在思念我親愛的丈夫，
我受的苦越多，就越發思念他！

Uncle Gyaltsen and Aunt Palden
叔父與嬸母

Chapter 2
PARTY

When Peta heard the distant sound of hooves on the road, she went out to check and quickly returned. "Mother, Uncle Thangme and Zesay's parents are here!" Everyone waited eagerly in the courtyard, and, soon, dressed in colourful silk robes with ornaments of gold, turquoise and coral, the guests arrived. The two men were in their forties. Zesay's mother looked rather plump and good-natured.

Thangme said, "Sister, we've come early to help you with tomorrow's party."

"I am so glad to have you here," said White Garland. "There isn't much to do, though. We are ready: the brown barley is brewed into beer, and the white ground into flour. Thopaga has gone to buy the meat. Thanks to you, we have enough money for everything. I am absolutely amazed at the huge crop you got out of my field, the Little Famine Carpet. Thank you again for all the hard work, and you sold the crop, too, at such a good price."

"That's fine," said Thangme, "Now, I'm sorry to say that the Garpon (Viceroy) can't come to your party. He was called to Lhasa suddenly, and has already left."

White Garland was disappointed for the Garpon was an

第二章
宴會

百德聽到馬路上遠遠傳來一陣馬蹄聲，她跑出去看了一下，很快又回來了。「媽媽，唐美伯父和澤思的父母來了！」所有人都在院子裏迫不急待地等着，客人們很快就到了，他們身穿華麗的絲綢禮服，帶有黃金、綠松石和珊瑚等配飾。這兩個男人都四十多歲。澤思的媽媽看上去有點豐滿，性情溫和。

唐美說：「妹妹，我們特意早點來幫你準備明天的聚餐。」

白花冠說：「儘管沒太多的事需要做，但你來了我很高興。我們已經準備好了：褐色的大麥已經釀成了酒，白色的小麥已磨成了麵。特巴加出去買肉去了。全靠你，我們的錢足以應付這一切。我那片貧瘠的土地上居然能收穫這麼多糧食，真是難以置信。真的謝謝你付出的汗水，而且糧食也被你賣了一個好價錢。」

「你太客氣了，」唐美說：「抱歉的是，總督不能來參加您的聚餐。他突然被調到拉薩去，並且已經走了。」

白花冠聽了有點失望，因為總督是她的一個重要親戚，

important connection on her side, and his presence would have lent much weight to her claims. She frowned. "I am more concerned because Thopaga hasn't yet returned. He left for the mountain three days ago to buy sheep directly from the shepherds. He'll drive the sheep to the butcher's outside the village. I wonder how he's coping – he hasn't been given such a big task before."

"You'll see him soon," Thangme said. "We've just passed him on the road. He's travelling slowly for his cart is heavy."

Not long after, Thopaga drove his horse-drawn cart into the courtyard. He called cheerfully, "Mother, I've bought eight sheep, two of them whole, the rest cut into sides, legs and chops, like you told me."

"Well done, young man!" Thangme said.

"Do we have the hearts, livers and intestines?" White Garland asked.

Thopaga shook his head. "I gave them all to the butcher as payment for his work."

White Garland said, "You should have kept some to use as an offering to the Gods." She turned to Thangme. "You see how young and inexperienced he is." They unloaded the cart and were soon busy preparing and dressing the meat.

White Garland spent a sleepless night waiting restlessly for the guests, who arrived by mid-morning. Aunt Palden and Uncle

他來了可以給她的主張撐腰。她皺了皺眉頭，說：「我有點擔心，因為特巴加還沒有回來。他三天前就上山了，想直接從牧羊人那裏買些羊。他會將羊群趕到村外的屠夫那裏。我想知道他辦得怎麼樣了，他從來沒有擔當如此重要的任務。」

「你很快就會看到他了，」唐美說。「我們剛才在路上碰到他了。他走得很慢，因為他車上的東西太重。」

不久，特巴加就駕着他的馬車來到了院子。他興奮地喊道：「媽媽，我買了八隻羊，其中兩只是完整的，其餘六隻都分割成了肉塊、腿和排骨，完全按照您的意思去辦的。」

「小伙子，幹得不錯！」唐美說。

「那些心、肝、腸拿回來了嗎？」白花冠問道。

特巴加搖了搖頭，說：「我把它們全給屠夫了，算是給他宰羊的報酬。」

白花冠說：「你應該拿一些回來祭神啊！」她回過頭來對唐美說。「你看，他太年輕，沒有經驗。」他們將東西從車上卸了下來，很快又忙着準備和處理這些肉。

白花冠渡過了一個不眠之夜，她心神不寧地等着客人到來。白卓姑媽和格列伯父帶着兒子們和隨從們來了，並被請

45

Gyaltsen came with an entourage of sons and supporters and were shown to the highest seats. It was painful for White Garland to see them resplendent in the gowns and ornaments that had belonged to her and her husband, while she and her children were so plainly dressed. Her only ornament was a purple *nambu*, a wide woollen sash she had woven herself. She usually wore a rope around her waist. Thopaga knelt down to present Uncle and Aunt with the white *hada,* his hands raised high above his head and his tongue stretched out, giving them the highest respect. White Garland then presented them with a whole sheep each, while the other guests received the gift of a quarter of sheep, a leg or several chops as was appropriate.

The feast began. When beer was flowing freely, White Garland stood up to make a speech. "Honourable guests, I want to explain to you the reason for this gathering. I have a few words to say regarding the last wishes of my late husband, Mila Sherab, the father of my son and daughter here. Although it is a matter already well known to you, please listen to my husband's will."

Thangme then stood up and read aloud the will.

White Garland followed this with, "Most of you were witnesses when my husband made his will. My children and I are deeply grateful to Uncle Gyaltsen and Aunt Palden for all they have done for us. Now that Thopaga has come of age and

到了最高的席位。白花冠看到他們穿着華麗的禮服和配飾，心裏很不是滋味，那些東西本該屬於她和她丈夫的，而現在，她和自己的孩子們穿得如此寒酸。她唯一的一件配飾就是一條紫色的腰帶，那是她自己編織的。通常她只在腰上纏一根繩子。特巴加跪了下來，向伯父和姑媽獻上了潔白的哈達，他將手高高舉過頭頂，並將舌頭伸出，向他們表示出最崇高的敬意。隨後，白花冠為他們兩個人呈上了一隻全羊，而其他的客人則相應得到了四分之一的羊、一條羊腿或幾塊羊排作為禮物。

宴會隨即開始了。當大家正喝在興頭上時，白花冠站起來說話。「各位尊敬的來賓，我想向大家說明一下這次聚餐的原因。我有幾句話要說是關於我的已故丈夫誰熱嘉參，也就是我兒子和女兒的父親最後的遺願，儘管大家對此都很了解，但請聽聽我丈夫的遺囑。」

唐美站起來將遺囑大聲地朗讀了一遍。

白花冠接着說：「我丈夫在立遺囑時，你們大部分人都目擊了這過程。我和我的孩子們都非常感激格列伯父和白卓姑媽為我們所做的一切。現在特巴加已長大成人，完全可以

47

can manage a household independently, I request that the property be restored to him. I also ask all of you to see to it that he marries Zesay, so they can make their home here, in accordance with the wishes of my late husband."

Uncle Gyaltsen said, "What are you talking about? Mila Sherab never owned property in his entire life. He had borrowed everything from us – the land, houses, animals, the gold and silver. He only returned it all at the hour of his death, repaying his large debt by handing over the property to its rightful owners – us. He didn't have a shred of wealth, not a yak of his own! How dare you say such things! Who wrote the will that you've just read aloud?"

"You ought to be thankful that we didn't leave miserable creatures like you to die of starvation," Aunt Palden screamed. "Expect no gratitude from wicked people, no matter how much you have done for them!"

They rose abruptly from their seats, shook their gowns and stamped their feet on the floor. "Come to think of it, this very house belongs to us. Out with you, you ungrateful things, out with you!" With that, they began to slap the faces of White Garland and her children with their long sleeves.

White Garland could only say, "Oh Mila Sherab, look how they are treating us! You said, 'I will be watching over you from the realm of the dead.' Surely now is the time to show your

獨立地掌管家產，我請求將財產交還給他。我還想讓大家親眼見證他與澤思婚禮，這樣他們就可以在這裏成家，這也是我已故丈夫的遺願。」

格列說：「你在說些什麼呢？誰熱嘉參在他的一生中從來沒有過什麼財產。他的一切都是從我們手裏借的——土地、房屋、禽畜以及金銀珠寶。他只不過是在臨死之前歸還了所有的東西而已，通過將財產移交給真正的所有者，也就是我們，以償還他欠下的巨額債務。他一點財富都沒有，連自己的一頭犛牛都沒有！你竟敢說出這樣的話！你們剛才讀的遺囑是誰寫的？」

「你們應該感謝我們沒有讓你們這群可憐的人餓死，」白卓姑媽尖叫起來。「不管你為這些壞人做了多少好事，你都別想他們會對你心存感激！」

他們突然從座位上站了起來，一邊甩着自己的禮服，一邊跺着腳。「我想起來了，這個房子其實是屬於我們的。你們這些不領情的東西滾出去！」說完，他們開始用長長的袖子抽打着白花冠和她孩子們的臉。

白花冠無可奈何地說：「誰熱嘉參，你看看他們是怎麼對待我們的！你曾經說過，『我會在天堂看着你們。』現在

power!" Weeping hysterically, she fell into a swoon. The children could only weep with her.

Thangme was shaking with anger, but he didn't dare start a fight for his side was greatly outnumbered. Uncle Gyaltsen had come prepared for fighting: his three sons and many supporters were armed with swords and knives. Aunt Palden said, "You want us to restore your wealth to you, but you seem to have a lot already. What a grand feast you are giving to your friends and neighbours. Don't you dare ask us again, because we haven't got anything that's yours. Even if we had, we'd never return it to you." She taunted White Garland. "Fight us if you are many and powerful. If you're too weak to fight, then curse us if you must, wretched orphans!" On these last words, Uncle and Aunt swept out with their troop of supporters.

Zesay's people and a few friends remained behind to console White Garland's family. They continued to drink what was left of the beer, saying, "It's useless to weep. Let's do something to help." They proposed to raise money for White Garland from all those who had attended the dinner, and offered to give their own share for a start.

"We should appeal to Uncle Gyaltsen and Aunt Palden again for a decent contribution," someone said. "The funds we raise should be used to send Mila Thopaga away to be educated."

正是你展示威力的時候了！」她歇斯底里地哭喊着，突然暈了過去。她的兩個孩子也只能陪她一起哭。

唐美氣得渾身發抖，但他不敢反抗，因為自己這邊勢單力薄。格列伯父來的時候已有所準備：他的三個兒子和許多擁護者都配備了刀劍。白卓姑媽說：「你想讓我們把你的財產還給你，但是你似乎已經很富有。你為朋友和鄰居們準備了如此豐盛的酒席。你還敢再向我們要？因為我們沒有一樣東西是屬於你的。即使我們有，也永遠不會還給你。」她對白花冠奚落道：「如果你人多力量大，就向我們開戰吧！如果你無力作戰，那就只能忍辱負重，可憐的孤兒！」說完最後這幾句話，伯父和姑媽帶着自己的一群擁護者離開了。

澤思一家和一些朋友留下來安慰白花冠。他們繼續喝着剩下的啤酒，他們邊喝邊說：「光哭是沒有用的。我們來做些力所能及的事吧。」他們提議所有參加聚餐的人為白花冠籌錢，並帶頭提供自己的股份，讓他們能夠重新開始。

「我們可以再次要求格列伯父和白卓姑媽拿出一筆較大數額的錢來，」有人說：「我們應該用籌來的資金送米拉特巴加出去求學。」

"Yes, let's do that," Thangme said to White Garland. "We'll send the boy away to learn something. And you and your daughter can come and live with me while you work your own field. We must do our best to put Uncle and Aunt to shame."

"My son must be educated, of course," White Garland replied, "but my children and I can't be a burden to you permanently, my brother. There is not the remotest possibility that Uncle and Aunt would restore any part of the legacy to us. If we ask them again we'll expose ourselves to worse insults and ill treatment than before. We'll remain here in this house and I'll work my field for a living."

So it was decided. The family's friends and relatives gave generously to help support them, and Thangme especially supplied White Garland with food so that she was not forced to beg or to serve others. He had wool for spinning and weaving brought to his house to save her from going door to door to ask for it. Peta earned her own spending money by doing whatever chores for others that she could find. By dint of hard work, they managed to scrape together a living, and be content with wearing rags and subsisting on very coarse food.

As promised, Mila Thopaga was sent away to Invisible Knoll, the school run by a Lama[1] of the Red Sect. But alone in her house, existing only on the kindness of others, no wonder a dark cloud of unhappiness hung constantly over White Garland.

「嗯，就這麼辦，」唐美對白花冠說：「我們要把這孩子送出去學點東西。你和你女兒可以來和我一起住，你還可以在自己的田裏幹活。我們必須竭盡全力讓伯父和姑媽感到羞愧。」

「當然，我兒子必須接受教育，」白花冠回答道：「但我和我的孩子們不能成為你永遠的負擔。伯父和姑媽絕不可能將任何遺產還給我們。如果我們再去問他們要，可能會比以前受到更大的污辱和惡劣的對待。我們還是留在這個房子裏，我會做些農活來維持生活的。」

事情就這麼決定了。家裏的朋友和親戚慷慨解囊支援他們，而唐美則專門為 白花冠提供食物，這樣她就不會被迫去乞討或去給其他人當僕人。他又在村子裏收集一些紡織用的羊毛，這樣她就不必挨家挨戶去問人家要了。百德也能為鄰人們做一些雜事，勉強維持自己的花費。通過辛勤勞動，他們勉強維持生活，儘管他們穿着破舊的衣服，吃着粗糙的食物，也倒算是安穩的度日。

正如當初所承諾的，米拉特巴加被送到了隱形山，這所學校由紅教的一個喇嘛經營。白花冠還依然孤獨地留在這個房子裏，僅靠親友們的好心幫助，難怪她總是一副愁雲莫展的模樣。

Mila and Zesay
米拉與澤思

Chapter 3

SCHOOL AT INVISIBLE KNOLL

The road to Invisible Knoll slipped off the edge of the plateau, slanting down several hundred feet to the bottom of a valley, before rising abruptly to a rocky hill. The hillock was named Invisible as it sat below the plateau, and was not noticeable from most parts of the village. The village school run by Lama Lugyat-Khan occupied the top of the knoll. The Lama and his family, together with a dozen pupils, lived in the few houses. Most of the children began their schooling at ten or twelve years old. As Mila was a late starter, he studied very hard to catch up and made rapid progress. He got on well with his Lama and, after a year, he was made Head Prefect of all the boys and assistant to the Lama.

The Lama taught reading, writing, prayers and, above all, the study of the Holy Texts. It was the Bonn[2] belief that the Texts contained all known worldly and celestial wisdom. Each day, the students got up very early for worship and meditation, then sat for instruction from the Lama. They had *zanba* before they returned to their rooms for study in the afternoon. Free time was time to walk and play games and cook their own food.

The Lama was also highly respected as a soothsayer.

第三章
隱形山上的學校

如果你要找到隱形山上的學校，你就要走到高原的邊緣，從一條陡峭的斜路走下數百呎的谷底，而後爬上一個獨立的小丘，學校就位於山頂。由於這座山坐落在高原之下，村子裏很多地方都看不到這座山，因此被大家稱為隱形山。這所鄉村學校由珞玡汗喇嘛經營。那裏有幾間房屋，裏面住着喇嘛和他的家人，還有十幾個學生。大部分孩子都是十歲至十二歲開始上學。由於米拉入學較晚，因此他學習非常刻苦，進步也非常快。他與校長相處融洽，一年後，他成為了所有男孩的頭並擔當校長的助手。

喇嘛教導的內容包括閱讀、寫作和祈禱，但最主要的是教大家學習聖典。按照波恩的信仰，聖典包含了所有天上人間的已知至理名言。每天，學生們都會早起默誦和祈禱，隨後接受喇嘛的教導，然後他們會吃一些奶茶，再回到房間繼續下午的學習。他們可以自由活動和玩遊戲，還可以自己做飯。

此外喇嘛善於占卜。村人在日常生活中都會要求他的指

People went to him for advice and help in their daily life. Before anything was undertaken, the soothsayer read the omens. Whether it was a matter of building a new house, going on a pilgrimage or getting married, he would ascertain the date when it would be auspicious for them to start. Through the use of astrological aspects, he gave advice on the naming of infants. He also advised on changes of name for adults after severe illness, or even to improve their luck. The Lama was much sought after.

Although the Lama didn't belong to the monastic order he was closely allied with the monastery. He was active in all the many religious festivals as a horn player, for he was a good musician. The students also participated in religious processions. On these days, Mila usually went home to see his mother and sister after the festival was over. He felt surprisingly uneasy during these home visits. When confronted with the hardship of his mother and sister, he felt somehow guilty but was completely helpless. He actually enjoyed school life for more reasons than one: his thirst for knowledge was being satisfied; he liked his youthful companions; and he was no longer subjected to the drudgery of field labour. He did his best to help out with the chores whenever he was home, but was always glad when it was time to leave for school again.

As Zesay's parents allowed her to visit him, she travelled two or three times each month to the school. She usually arrived

點。在做任何事情之前，占卜者都會了解一下相關的徵兆。不管是蓋新房、去朝聖，還是結婚，他都必須先確認一下他們在哪個日子開始會比較吉利。他還提供一些起名的建議，別人常請他使用占星術為新生兒起名字。此外，成年人在經歷大病之後想改名時，甚至只是想改名來增加點運氣時，他也可以建議一些名字。

喇嘛與修道院關係密切，儘管他不是個寺廟的僧人。由於他愛好音樂，他經常在許多宗教活動上擔當吹長笛。學生們也會參加宗教活動。在這段時間，米拉常常會在活動結束後回家看望自己的媽媽和妹妹。這些回家的歷程，居然讓他感到有些不自在。當面對他母親和妹妹的艱難生活時，他感到有一點犯罪感，但卻完全幫不上忙。也難怪他：他喜歡學校生活；他對知識的渴求得到了滿足；他喜歡那幫年輕的同伴；並且他再也不用做田地勞作那份苦差事了。每次他在家時，總是儘量多做家務，不過一旦要回到學校時，他也總是非常高興。

澤思的父母允許她去看望米拉，因此，她每個月都會去學校。她經常下午到那裏，那時米拉會有一些自由活動的時

in the afternoon when school was in recess and Mila had some free time. She brought food, as she knew that the students' fare was meager. Often, Mila and Zesay went walking down the valley to the pond where they sat and talked until dusk. Mila always looked forward to her visits. She was very encouraging and he was proud of her loveliness. One day, she said, "Do not worry about being poor. Your family came penniless to our village and got wealthy by trading. You can do the same. Surely, it's in your blood!"

"I don't think I've got what it takes to be a successful trader," Mila said. "I'd rather be a lama, for that is also in my blood. My great-grandfather, Dotun, was a lama. He was well known for his power to ward off a hailstorm, to protect children from vampires and ghosts, and other things as well."

Zesay asked, "Do you want to be a village lama, like your great-grandfather, or your schoolmaster?"

"Oh, more than that!" Mila said. "Magic is also an important aspect of my family heritage. Our family name was originally Khyungpo. My lama ancestor, Khyungpo Josay, was famous for his power to heal the sick, and he exorcised people possessed by demons. One man was possessed by a demon that couldn't be driven away. They sent for Josay to do the exorcism.

間。她常常會帶些食物，因為她知道學生們的伙食較差。米拉和澤思經常沿着山谷走到池塘，然後坐在那裏聊天，直到夜幕降臨。米拉總是盼望着她的到來。她總是給他帶來勇氣，他對她的魅力感到很自豪。有一天，她說：「不用擔心現在很窮。你的家族在剛來我們村的時候也是一貧如洗，他們靠做生意走上了致富之路。你也可以做到。當然，你的血統裏就有這種能力！」

「我覺得我不具備成為成功商人的潛質，」米拉說。「我寧願當一名喇嘛，這也是我血統的一部分。我的曾祖父就是一名喇嘛。他能夠阻擋冰雹、保護孩子們免受吸血鬼和幽靈的殘害，並具有其他方面的一些魔力，因此遠近聞名。」

澤思問：「你想在村裏當一名像你曾祖父那樣的喇嘛，還是當一名像你校長那樣的喇嘛呢？」

「哦，不僅僅像他們一樣！」米拉說。「魔法也是我家族傳統的重要部分。我們最初的姓是窘不。我的喇嘛祖先侯色窘不就很有名氣，他醫術高超，並能幫人驅魔除怪。有一個人一直擺脫不了魔鬼的控制。他們就把這個人送到侯色那裏去驅魔。最終那個魔鬼感到非常恐懼，哭喊着：「『Apa！

In the end, the demon was so terrorised that it cried out, 'Apa! Ama! Mila! Mila!' (Oh man, you are my father, you are my mother!) The demon begged for his life and was allowed to depart. From that day, Josay was known as Mila in recognition of his magic. That is why our family name was changed from Kyungpo to Mila."

"Once I saw the famous Lama Bari in Tingri, a village nearby," Zesay said. "He was walking under a huge yellow umbrella, dressed in colourful silks and surrounded by many disciples and followers. Some of them walked in pairs in front of him, blowing trumpets. Some blew conch shells or flutes, and others beat on drums and cymbals. Then he was seated on a throne and served with tea or beer. He attracted a large crowd wherever he went and collected their offerings in large quantities. Your mother would be so proud of you if you became an eminent lama. Your relatives would also benefit."

Mila knew that was not what he wanted, but didn't have the heart to disappoint her. He saw how lovely she looked, sitting by the pond with the setting sun behind her, and sang her this song:

In this valley full of meadows, greensward and trees,
Above me, the school where my dear companions stay,
Before me, Zesay, sitting by a crystal clear pond,
Insects are humming on floating lotus with fragrant scent,
On the sandy shore, waterfowls arch their necks to see,
Beautiful birds are singing a chorus in the trees,
Swaying branches are dancing in the cool breeze,

Ama！米拉！米拉！』（主啊，你是我的父母！）魔鬼向他求饒，才得以脫身。從那時候開始，人們開始認可侯色的魔法，尊稱他為米拉。這就是我的姓由窘不改為米拉的原因。」

「我曾經在鄰村丁惹看到過一個很有名的巴厘喇嘛，」澤思說。「他當時在一把很大的黃傘下走着，身穿彩色的絲綢，周圍有許多信徒和隨從。有些人吹着喇叭成隊地走在他前面。還有一些人吹着螺號或長笛，其他人則打着鼓和鐃鈸。當時他坐在寶座上，有人替他端茶遞酒。不管他走到哪，都會吸引一大群人，收到大量的禮物。如果你成為一名出色的喇嘛，你母親一定會為你感到非常自豪。你的親戚也會因此受益。」

米拉知道那不是他想要的，但他不想讓她感到失望。她看上去是多麼地可愛，坐在池塘邊，一輪落日映襯在身後，他一邊看着她，一邊給她唱着歌：

在這個山谷裏，到處都是牧場、草地和樹木，
在我上面，是我親愛的同伴所在的學校，
在我前面，澤思正坐在清澈的池塘邊，
昆蟲在漂浮的蓮花上嗡嗡叫，溢出芳香，
在沙灘上，水禽彎着脖子在張望，
成群小鳥在樹叢中歌唱，
搖擺的樹枝在寒冷的微風中跳舞，

From a distance, flute notes of the homing herdsmen,
From all I survey, you are the loveliest, gentle Zesay,
Mirrored on the water,
Behind you, the glorious sun-set.

Several weeks later, there was a school holiday. As this was an auspicious day, the Lama was invited to perform the naming ceremony of a newborn from a wealthy family, and he asked Mila to accompany him. The Lama was in a good mood as the family had shown him much respect and loaded him with gifts, making him the guest of honour during the feast and plying him with drinks. When Mila had had his share of feasting, his Lama asked him to leave first, carrying the presents received. Mila went off in high spirits – he had been drinking, and his singing during the feast had been much admired. He felt an irresistible urge to keep on singing, to proudly show off his fine voice. As he walked, he sang this song:

My heart is glad, that to-day
Under the canopy of happiness,
You gift offering and feast making men and women,
My Lama and I have met in a gathering.
To you all, joyful tidings will be announced.
My revered Lama is in good health,
Are you, generous friends in good health?

The way to Invisible Knoll passed right in front of Mila's own home, and he was still singing as he neared the house. White Garland was toasting some barley in the kitchen; she could

在遠方，回家的牧人吹着笛，
在我看到的一切事物中，你是最可愛的，溫柔的澤思，
你倒映在水中，
身後有一輪絢爛的落日。

幾個星期以後，學校放假了。由於這是吉日，喇嘛受一家有錢人之約去為新生兒舉行起名儀式，他要求米拉隨他同行。喇嘛心情很不錯，因為這家人非常尊重他，並給了他很多禮物，在席間一直把他當貴賓對待，不停地給他敬酒。當米拉享用完盛宴後，喇嘛要求他先行一步，把收到的禮物帶回去。米拉興高采烈地走了——他酒足飯飽，並且他在席間的歌聲也得到了大家的高度讚揚。他按捺不住內心的喜悅，繼續唱着歌，驕傲地展示他優美的嗓音。他一邊走，一邊唱着：

今天我心情真高興，
在歡樂氣氛的籠罩下，
豐富的禮物和盛宴讓男女老少，
我的喇嘛和我能夠相聚在一起，
令人興奮的消息將向所有人宣佈。
我敬愛的喇嘛身體健康，
啊，慷慨的朋友，你們也身體健康嗎？

去隱形山正好會路過米拉自家的門前，在他離家越來越近的時候，他仍然沒有停止唱歌。白花冠正在廚房烤一些大麥；她幾乎不敢相信自己的耳朵，但她不會聽錯米拉特有的

hardly believe her ears, but Mila's distinctive voice could not be mistaken. Still, how could Mila be in such a joyful singing mood, she wondered, when their family situation was so desperate, and she felt so unhappy? When she looked out and saw that it really was Mila Thopaga, she was dumbfounded. She immediately dropped the roasting-whisk and let the barley burn in the pan, picked up a rod in her right hand, a handful of ashes in her left, and rushed out. She ran towards Mila, jumping down some steps and sliding part of the way down the slope.

When she finally caught up with him, she threw the ashes in his face and struck his head with the rod several times. "Oh, Mila Sherab, see what sort of a son I have!" she exclaimed. "Surely, it can't be your blood flowing in this rascal. Oh heaven, what have we come to!" She fell to the ground in a faint.

Peta ran out and said, "Brother, what have you done? Take care of Mother!" She started to weep and this brought Mila to his senses. He was also in tears and they both kept calling piteously to their mother.

After a short while, she came to. Looking fixedly at Mila, she said, "Son, do you really feel merry enough to sing? As for me, I think we are the most miserable creatures on earth. I am so full of sorrow that the only thing I can do is to weep." Then the three of them wept loudly together.

"Mother, you are right," Mila said, "but don't take it too

嗓音。她心想，他們家境況淒涼，而且她感到如此悲傷，而米拉卻還能唱出這麼歡快的歌曲。她朝外面看了一下，發現真的是米拉特巴加，她感到目瞪口呆。她馬上放下烘烤义子，任由大麥在平底鍋裏焦燒，右手操起一根木棍，左手抓了一把灰，衝了出去。她跳下幾階臺階，沿着斜坡滑了一段，朝米拉跑去。

她終於追上了他，順手將灰拋在他的臉上，然後又用木棍對着他的腦袋打了幾下。「哎呀，誰熱嘉參，你看看，我怎麼有這樣一個兒子！」她喊道。「是的，這小子身上不可能有你的血統。噢，天啊，我們什麼時候才能出頭啊！」說完後她暈倒在地上。

百德跑了出來說：「哥哥，你到底做了些什麼？好好照顧媽媽！」她開始哭了起來，這讓米拉也感到傷感，淚流滿面。他們一起可憐地呼喊着自己的母親。

過了一會兒，她醒了過來。她目不轉睛地盯着米拉說：「兒子，你真的覺得很開心，忍不住要唱歌嗎？在我看來，我們是世界上最可憐的人。我的內心充滿了悲痛，每天除了哭還是哭。」說完，他們三個人一起大聲痛哭了起來。

「媽媽，你說的對，」米拉說：「但不要太放在心上。

much to heart. I solemnly promise to obey you in whatever you wish. What is your will?"

"I want revenge!" White Garland said fiercely. "I would like to see you in a coat of mail, mounted on a steed, stamping over the bodies of our enemies. But that is impossible to achieve and, besides, would be too dangerous for you. My wish is that you should learn the black arts thoroughly, so that you can kill these enemies of ours. I want you to destroy your uncle and aunt, who have caused us so much misery. Let their roots be cut off! See if you can do this for me!"

Mila felt torn apart by his mother's words – he knew that he owed her his life. "I promise faithfully to do my best to fulfill your wish," he said, "but you will have to provide me with the means. I would need to pay fees to the Gurus of the Black Arts, expenses on the road, as well as living expenses while I'm studying. How is this possible, if we are so poor?"

"I will find a way," vowed White Garland.

Mila returned to the school with the presents and waited to hear from his mother. Committed to the promise she'd made, White Garland sold half of the field she had inherited, called "Little Famine Carpet", in exchange for a splendid turquoise and several gold pieces. She also managed to acquire two loads of raw sugar and two loads of madder for dyeing, which could be sold by Mila to defray the travelling expenses. Mila loaded the sugar and madder on a pony, secured the gold pieces and the

我鄭重向你保證，以後堅決按照你的願望去做事。你的願望是什麼呢？」

「我想報仇！」白花冠狠狠地說。「我想看到你身穿盔甲、騎上戰馬、踐踏在我們敵人的身體上。但這不太可能實現，而且對你來說也太危險。我的願望是：你能徹底學會魔法，這樣你就可以消滅我們的敵人。我希望你消滅你的伯父和姑媽，他們是令到我們如此窮困的罪魁禍首。斷絕他們的根基！看看你是否能為我做到這些！」

米拉感到自己被母親的話撕扯成了兩半——他知道自己的生命是母親給的。「我保證竭盡全力實現你的願望，」他說，「但你將不得不給我一些錢。我需要給魔法老師交錢，路上也有一些花銷，另外在學習期間還要一些生活費。我們現在這麼窮，怎麼可能承擔這些？」

「我會想出辦法的，」白花冠發誓說。

米拉帶着禮物回到學校，等着他母親的消息。白花冠履行了自己的承諾，她將自己繼承的「一小塊貧瘠的土地」中的一半出售了，換來了華麗的綠松石和幾枚金幣。她還設法買了兩擔粗糖和兩擔染色用的西草染料，可供米拉賣了去支付旅行的費用。米拉將粗糖和染料拴在馬上，把金幣和綠松

turquoise under his clothing, and set out on his quest. His mother accompanied him a considerable way, serving him with food and drink at every resting point.

Finally, the moment came for their farewells. In a low voice broken with sobs, White Garland gave her son a parting admonition. "My dear son, you are not seeking to learn magic for fame or fortune. Yours is a case of desperate necessity: consider the wretched state we are in and the wrongs we have suffered." She clutched his hands tightly. "You must return and wreak damage in this village, create great destruction, to punish these people who have trampled on us. If you come home without the power to carry this out, I swear that I will kill myself before you!"

She walked away, and Mila began his journey alone, but he could not bear to part from her. He looked back again and again, and tears flowed freely down his cheeks. As Mila was her only son, White Garland suffered no less. They kept looking back at each other as long as they were within sight. Mila had an almost irresistible urge to run to her and embrace her once more, but conquered it with a super-human effort. He would later find that his great sorrow at parting with his mother had been a premonition, for he would never see her alive again. A few days later, the rumour spread far and wide that the son of White Garland had gone away to learn magic in order to avenge the wrongs done to his family.

石藏在衣服下面，朝着自己的目標出發了。他的母親陪伴他走了很長一段路，在每個休息地點為他提供食物和酒水。

最後，他們不得不告別了。白花冠在臨別時哽咽地對兒子說道：「我親愛的兒子。你出去學魔法不是為了出名，也不是為了發財。這是你在絕望的情況下必需採取的措施：想想我們所處的悲慘境遇，以及我們所承受的不公平待遇。」她緊緊地抓住他的手。「你必須回到這個村子裏來為我們所受的傷害報仇，帶來極大的毀滅，以懲罰那些粗暴地對待我們的人。如果你回家後沒有能力做到這些，我發誓我會在你面前自殺的！」

她走了，米拉開始獨自繼續他的旅程，但他不能承受與她離別。他一步三回頭，任由眼淚順着臉頰流下來。白花冠同樣也很痛苦，米拉是她唯一的兒子。他們還在視線範圍內的時候，一直都在回頭張望對方。米拉有一種無法抑制的欲望想再跑回去擁抱她，但還是無情地克制住了。他後來發現自己有一種不祥的預感，他懷疑自己可能再也見不到她了。幾天後，謠言很快就傳開了：白花冠的兒子為了報復家人承受的冤屈而出去學魔法了。

Chapter 4

RED MOUNTAIN FAERIE

Mila followed the main road until he came to the next town, where he sold his pony and the dyestuff to a rich man. He was paid in gold coins, which he hid under his shirt in a cloth-belt tied to his body. He stayed several days at an inn, asking the townspeople if there was a Lama in the region, one able to teach Black Magic that dealt out death and destruction. "No," everyone replied, "there is no such teacher here." He decided to go to the Province of U, where many more people lived, to make further enquiries. To get there, he first had to climb Red Mountain.

Mila began walking at daybreak. As he gradually came near Red Mountain, he was amazed by its magnificent russet colour. By late afternoon, he'd reached Rock Jewel Valley. Needing shelter for the night, he explored the surrounding slopes and luckily found a rock cavern with a sandy floor. He laid down his sack, went to collect an armful of firewood, and then walked to a small stream for some water. He had brought tea, flour, and a small pot with him and, using these, he cooked his evening meal, and then enjoyed his tea perched on a rock overlooking the valley below. Dusk was gathering, but he could still see the silvery river threading through the green valley and

第四章
紅山女仙

米拉沿着大路一直走到最近的城市。在那裏他把小馬和染布料賣給一個有錢人。他把得到的金幣藏在布袋裏繫在身上。而後他在一家客棧住了幾天。

他到處問人那裏可找到懂巫術的喇嘛，為了他想學會能殺人及毀滅的黑魔法。每個人的回答都是「沒有！哪裏會有這樣的老師啊！」於是他決定到較多人居住的 U 鄉去進一步查詢。

首先他要爬過紅山。米拉在黎明出發，走向宏偉褐色的紅山。越走近景色越令他驚嘆！午後他來到「寶石谷」，探索周圍的斜坡，他幸運的找到一個乾淨的山洞，洞底鋪滿細沙，這就是他棲息過夜的地方。他放下包袱，收集一堆柴火，走到一條小溪取水。把帶來的茶葉、麵粉用一個小鍋開始煮晚餐。享用餐時，他坐在岩石上俯瞰山谷。夜幕低垂，他仍然可看見一條銀線般的河，流過深綠色的山谷，成群的鳥兒

flocks of birds returning to their nests. When it was finally dark, he turned in for the night and was soon fast asleep.

He woke with a start, hearing a strange whistling sound, and felt a strong gust of air blowing over him. Was he dreaming? But when he opened his eyes, light was streaming out from a cleft in the wall. The cave walls had opened up to reveal a path in bright sunlight. Twenty feet away, a red man wearing the fur of a snow leopard rode towards him slowly on the back of a black musk deer. Leading the deer was the most beautiful girl Mila had ever seen. She wore an elegant embroidered gown, and strings of coral and turquoise necklaces. The man went by, brushing Mila's shoulder, and disappeared. Fear rose inside Mila; he got up quickly to escape from the cave but, after running a few steps, he was suddenly grabbed by the heel and pulled down. The beautiful girl had changed into a huge red dog and was holding onto his ankle with her teeth.

In despair, Mila hid his face for a few moments, but finally plucked up enough courage to turn and face his captor. He started singing in a clear voice:

In the East, the rising sun chases the pale moon away,
To gladden all hearts, he sends out his golden ray,
May Rehu's black clouds not stop his blessing!

In the West, by the shining glacier, the snow leopard is prancing,
He is wearing a coat so splendid, all the beasts admire their king,
May a trap not be laid for him at the Mountain's edge!

歸巢了。當夜色降臨時，他回到洞穴，很快的就進入了夢鄉。

　　他突然被驚醒了，他聽見奇怪的口哨聲，又有一陣強風吹向他。他以為在夢中，但他睜開眼睛時，一道光從壁縫裏透出來，有一條路徑從打開了的洞壁通出去，外面陽光普照。不遠處，一個全身紅色的男子，穿着雪豹袍，騎在黑麝背上，正向他緩緩走來。拉麝的女郎，是<u>米拉</u>從未見過的絕色美女。她身穿優雅的刺繡長裙，頸上戴着用珊瑚和綠松石鑲的項鍊。這男子和<u>米拉</u>擦身而過時消失了。<u>米拉</u>突然感到很恐怖，他迅速起身想逃出洞穴。但他只走了幾步，他的腳跟突然被抓住，向下扯。轉瞬間，漂亮的女孩變成一隻巨大紅色的母狗，正咬着他的足踝不放！

　　<u>米拉</u>絕望的把臉埋在地上，但只一會兒，他就鼓起勇氣來，轉身面對着他的劫持者。他用清晰的聲音唱起歌來。

在東方，初升的太陽趕走了蒼白的月亮，
他發出金色的光芒，人人都心情開朗。
但願<u>熱呼拉</u>的黑雲不會阻擋他的祝福！

在西方的冰川，雪豹正在奔騰，
牠穿着華麗的皮袍，
所有野獸都羨慕牠們的王。
但願牠不會跌入山邊的陷阱！

In the forest of the South, proudly prowls the striped tiger,
To all beasts in this green domain, he is the mighty ruler,
May he not be hunted when he goes on the narrow paths!

In the North, high above the icy crags, the vulture soars in play,
This noble bird has a Buddha heart and will never take live prey,
When he returns to his nest, may he not be met with a flying arrow!

Through the Red Mountain valley, Mila is making his way to his teacher,
Doing so, he is obedient to the dearest wish of his sorrowful mother,
May his journey not be in vain because of you, oh illusory maid!

The girl resumed her human appearance and said, "My name is Veda. I play alone in the shining glacier. I am pleased that you've come to this cave, and yet, I am also not pleased. I appear to you because I am glad of your companionship, and I am not lonely anymore. But I hold you down because I'm angry that you've broken into our sanctified cave. I shall release you only if you can answer this riddle:

> *It's not a tiger, but it has stripes,*
> *It's not a leopard, but it has contrasting colours,*
> *It's not a yak in heat with its mate, but it sucks,*
>
> *What is it?"*

Mila sighed with relief and answered, "It's a bee!"

Her laugh was like jingling silver bells. For a moment, her form glowed in rainbow threads of light before disappearing.

Mila didn't try to sleep again; instead, he sat and meditated for the rest of the night. When it was light, he resumed his journey and, where the path turned, he looked back and saw

在南方的森林，條紋斑斕的猛虎正在潛行，
在這綠色的國度裏，牠是所有野獸的王。
當牠走上狹路時，但願牠不會遭遇獵人。

在北方，冰封的峭壁上，禿鷹正在飛翔。
這崇高的鳥兒有顆慈悲的心，
永不獵食活物。
但願牠不會遇上飛箭。

米拉走過紅山谷，
去尋找一位能傳授他的老師，
為了服從他母親傷心的指令。
但願他不會徒勞無功，
只因為妳啊，虛幻的仙女！

女孩恢復她人的型相，說道：「我叫維達，我獨自在閃亮的冰川裏玩。我很高興你來陪我，我不再孤單了。我按住你是因為你闖進而破壞了我們神聖的洞穴。只要你能解答我的謎語，我就釋放你！」

牠不是一隻老虎，
但牠長有斑紋。
牠不是豹子，
牠卻有着鮮明對比的顏色。
牠不是發情的公犛牛和母牛，卻常用嘴吸啜，
牠是什麼?

米拉舒了口氣，答道：「是蜜蜂！」

她的笑聲像一陣清脆的銀鈴，然後不再是血肉之軀，變成霓虹光線描繪的人形，漸漸消失了。

米拉不敢再入睡，他打坐到天亮，而後他再次上路。當

Veda standing outside the cave. He pushed on, but whenever he looked back, he could see her behind a rock, or half hidden by a bush. At the bottom of Red Mountain, as he was about to ford a stream, he heard her calling his name. He did not look back again but went steadily on his way.

他回頭時，他看到<u>維達</u>在洞外，他一直向前走。但每當他回頭時，他總是見到她，半躲在岩石後，或在灌木叢中。當他走到<u>紅山</u>山腳，正要涉水過溪流的時候，他聽到她在呼喚他的名，但他沒有回頭看，他穩步向前走，離開了<u>紅山</u>。

Outlaws in the Desert. Mila and Desert Tribesmen
米拉與沙漠強盜

Chapter 5

SORCERER OF THE DESERT

Mila followed the main road to the wide plain of Tingri. Walking through well-tended meadows and fields, he saw more and more travellers on horseback or driving mules packed with cargo. In the distance soared the gleaming golden roof of a temple. He had marched for seven days and was very glad to arrive, making his devotions by adding a stone to the cairn at the roadside before entering through the wide town gate that spanned the valley bottom. Roadside stalls were selling sweets and delicacies that made his mouth water, but he couldn't afford to buy any.

On top of a hill was the most splendid monastery he had ever seen, with numerous gilded pinnacles rising above the shrine. The monks lived in stone houses within a large compound and, as usual, the common people's houses of mud-brick were built behind the hill, protected from wind. Mila walked through the inner city, which was full of shops with merchants' goods overflowing into the streets. One could buy everything there, including clothing and fabric, provisions and jewellery. The well-dressed crowd talked, laughed and bargained noisily, but Mila felt too shy to mix with them, not least because the prices of the goods were prohibitive.

第五章
沙漠的巫師

米拉沿着大路來到丁幾利廣闊的平原。經過肥沃的農田和放牧的草原，越來越多人在趕路，有騎馬的人，趕驢的，驢子背負重包。不遠處可以看見寺廟閃亮的屋頂。在進入橫跨山谷底的城門前，他加了塊石在路旁的瑪尼堆裏作為他的奉獻。路邊攤販賣的糖果和美點，令他垂涎三尺，可惜他都買不起。

山頂有一座最輝煌的寺廟，神社頂還有許多鍍金的小尖塔。喇嘛們住在大院子裏的石屋，普通百姓住的泥磚房子，都蓋在山後能遮擋風的地方。米拉在城內走着，街上都是商店，貨物溢滿整條街道。幾乎任何東西都可以買到：衣服、布料、日常必需品、甚至珠寶、首飾，應有盡有。衣著光鮮的人群講話聲、笑聲、討價還價聲，充斥着整個空間。但貨物的價太貴了，使米拉裹足不敢參與在人群中。

He found lodging at an inexpensive small inn, but as the monks there were rather important-looking, Mila felt too timid to approach them. He waited until the morning bustle was over and most of the guests had gone out before striking up a conversation with the innkeeper. The friendly old man said, "I don't know of any sorcerer. Sorcery is strictly forbidden in this region, as we are under the jurisdiction of a Cathedral of the Yellow Sect. You are well advised not to broach this subject with anyone, otherwise you'll certainly get into trouble."

Seeing how lost and downcast Mila looked, the innkeeper volunteered more information. "The nomads in the desert believe in sorcery. I have heard of a terrible sorcerer in the desert who can kill people from hundreds of miles away and can call up hailstorms."

Mila brightened. "Where can I find this great sorcerer?"

"Nobody knows where he lives," the old man said mysteriously. "If you go looking for him in the desert, he'll know. He only sees those with the right karma."

Overnight, Mila carefully thought through his situation. He would not ask the townspeople about sorcery anymore, in view of the innkeeper's warning, and staying longer would only lead to more expense. He made up his mind to go into the desert the next morning. He'd make his devotions there and the sorcerer would certainly come to him.

他找到一家價格便宜的小旅館，但裏面的喇嘛派頭十足，米拉有點羞怯，不敢靠近。他等到差不多客人都離開了，氣氛平靜了，他和店家開始攀談起來。友善的老人說：「我不認識任何魔法師。在我們黃教的管轄下這地區是禁止魔法的；我勸你不要對其他人提起這事，否則你一定會惹上麻煩！」

店家看到米拉沮喪的樣子，自願給他多一點資料。「沙漠裏的遊牧人相信巫術。我聽說在沙漠裏有一個可怕巫師可以在百哩外殺人，還可以召令雹暴。」

米拉臉露喜色。「那裏能夠找到這個偉大的巫師？」

「沒有人知道他住哪裏。」老人神秘的說着。「如果你去沙漠找他，他一定會知道。他只會出來見那些有緣人。」

米拉通宵仔細思量他現在的情況。考慮到店家的警告，他不會再問城裏人關於巫術了。住得越久，費用越多，他下決心第二天一早進沙漠。奉獻了虔誠，他肯定巫師一定會為他而來的。

On his way to the desert, Mila walked across a wide, undulating plateau. In the clear light, he could see for miles – the high peaks and shining glaciers that seemed so near were actually far away. Several times he had to wade through the icy water of a swift running stream and occasionally there were showers of hail. The weather often changed abruptly, from warm sunshine to a freezing snowstorm. The country seemed completely deserted, except for a small herd of wild goats, but the few skeletons of animals scattered on the ground indicated shepherds made good use of the pastureland in warmer weather.

Hidden in the landscape were the small stone enclosures built by nomadic herdsmen to protect their tents from winds and storms. He sought these out for shelter at night. He camped in the open, behind the stone walls, lighting fires of yaks' dung that he had collected. The sheepskin cloak provided by his mother proved to be extremely useful, serving as a coat in the daytime and as a blanket to curl up in at night. For food, he depended on the bag of meal that he was carrying; but after five days in the wilderness, it was nearly exhausted, which worried him. He didn't feel lonely but was strangely calm and at peace in the vast empty space.

As he walked, he ruminated on his past. Life at home had always been stormy, and he could hardly remember the good old days when his father was alive, for he'd died when Mila was

米拉在沙漠裏走着，經過起伏的高原。天色如此晴朗，看似接近的高山和閃亮的冰川，其實都在幾哩以外。他也曾涉水走過結冰，湍急的河流，偶而還有陣陣冰雹。天氣往往在不到一小時內，從陽光普照，突然變爲暴雪嚴寒。就因爲天氣的變幻無常，這鄉下裏除了少數的野山羊外，看似完全無生物；但從撒落在地上的動物骸骨，卻説明這草原在暖和的天氣裏是充分的被牧羊人利用的。

隱藏在景觀裏有些小石墻圍，是遊牧人建來遮擋風暴以保護帳篷的。米拉尋找這些牆圍，是他過夜露宿的地方。他燃起先前收集的犛牛糞，蓋上媽媽給他帶着、白天穿起的羊皮披風。在曠野五天，帶來的食物差不多要用盡了，這令他非常擔心。這一片巨大的空間，是那麼出奇的平靜、安詳，他並不覺得寂寞。

他一面走着，一面反覆思考……在家風風雨雨的生活，幾乎想不起他爸爸在生時過的好日子。他爸爸在米拉七歲時，就已經過世了。他只想到他媽媽淚流滿臉和她的懇求、

only seven. He thought of the parting with his mother, her tearful face and her entreaties, the pressure of her relentless passion, her sufferings at the loss of their fortune, and her anger at Aunt and Uncle and the villagers. He felt her pain and his heart went out to her, but in all honesty, he was enjoying the feeling of escape, of freedom. She had made him swear to avenge the great wrong done to her, to learn black magic and wreak revenge on his evil aunt and uncle. In reality, he was terrified of black magic. He had never even killed an animal by his own hand, as the taking of life was sinful and strictly forbidden. When he made his devotions he asked for divine guidance, even a miracle, to solve this dilemma.

Mila got up the next morning feeling down-hearted because his food was exhausted and he could not travel further without provisions. He doubted he had lost his way, and so pushed on regardless. Suddenly he saw the black dots of a caravan on the horizon. Was it a mirage? No, the black dots moved and stopped. After two hours of rapid walking, he met up with the caravan drivers, who were surprised to find him alone in such wilderness and took him in. Mila was very glad to be ladling down hot soup and sleeping in a tent again.

The caravan was on a journey of combined pilgrimage and trading. They were herding hundreds of cattle and sheep to sell in the market near Mount Kailas. Each day they travelled for

她盛怒無情的壓力、她失去財富承受的痛苦、以及她對姑媽、伯父、鄉親的怒氣。他感受到她的痛苦，心快要奔向她了；但確實地說，他很享受現在逃脫的自由。她要他起誓，學習魔法來報復她所受的冤屈和摧毀他邪惡的姑媽和伯父。實際上，他害怕黑魔法。他從來沒有親手殺過一隻動物，況且這也是陷入罪惡和違禁的事。他祈禱，請求指示，甚至期望有奇跡幫他解決這個難題。

第二天早上他醒來，感到非常沮喪，沒有食物進食，體力不濟，怎麼前進！他懷疑迷路了，但他還是不顧一切的推進。突然他看見地平綫上有一行像車隊的黑點，不會是海市蜃樓吧？啊，那行黑點會移動！他疾步的向着黑點走，大約花了兩小時，終於見到車隊。車夫們看到他獨自一個人在曠野中，都覺得很驚奇，接着收留了他。有熱湯喝，有帳篷睡，米拉感覺不錯。

車隊行程包括朝聖和貿易。他們趕着幾百頭的牛、羊要到神山附近的市集去賣。車隊每天大約走四哩路便會紮營，

about four miles before they pitched camp and let the animals out to graze. Mila helped with the milking and other chores, and was a welcome guest. At night they sat by the campfire, talked and drank beer. The herdsmen told Mila, "We have travelled this route back and forth throughout the years, and we know of no sorcerer in the desert. You should go to Mount Kailas, which is the destination for thousands of pilgrims from all parts of Tibet, as well as from Nepal and India. This is the Holy Place for all the Sects, including the Bonn Sect. Everyone knows the Bonn gurus are sorcerers. If you make enquiries there, you'll certainly find yourself a teacher of black magic."

A pilgrimage to the Holy Mountain! Mila would be following the footsteps of his father and grandfather before him. Such an auspicious pilgrimage would certainly lead him to the right guru. However, the caravan was moving too slowly, so he decided to go on his own, despite the warnings of the herdsmen. They had banded together for protection against the Kampas, outlaw tribesmen who regularly robbed and killed the pilgrims in their territory. Mila had actually seen several dark-clothed men on horseback trying to follow them but they were driven off by the herdsmen.

Several hours after Mila made off on his own, he saw again the same group of men on horseback, accompanied by fierce dogs. He tried his best to be invisible by pressing his body

放牧牲口。米拉幫忙擠奶和幹活,是個受歡迎的客人。晚上
大家圍坐在營火邊,一邊談話一邊喝酒。牧人告訴米拉:「我
們整年在這條道上來回的走,從來也沒聽說過這沙漠上有巫
師。你應該去神山,那裏有成千名朝聖者來自西藏各部落、
尼泊爾及印度。那裏是所有宗派的聖地,包括波恩宗派。大
家都知道波恩大師們都是巫師,如果你去那裏詢問,你肯定
會找到老師教你黑魔法的!」

去神山朝聖!米拉跟隨他父親,祖父的足跡。這樣吉祥
的朝聖必定會帶領他找到合適的大師。然而車隊的步伐太
慢,他沒有理會牧人的警告,決定獨自上路。車隊聯合起來
目的是爲了抵抗甘巴族人、亡命歹徒在這領域裏搶劫和殺死
朝聖者。他們也曾被幾個騎馬的黑衣人跟蹤,不過都被牧人
趕走了。

米拉幾小時的獨行中,他又遇上了同一幫黑衣人和他們
兇猛的狗。他將身體貼緊在岩石上,希望這幫人看不到他,

against a rock, hoping that the band would ride on, but they stopped and came towards him. Surrounded by the tall dark men, Mila collapsed with fear and almost fainted, terrified of their ugly dogs that barked and foamed at the mouth.

The leader gave a command and one tall rider dismounted. With one hand, he plucked Mila from the ground, looked him fiercely in the eye and shook him violently, then suddenly turned him upside down. Mila's small knife, his comb, several coins, and odds and ends scattered from his pockets. The man let go and dropped Mila to the ground like a bag of rags and bones that he kicked at with the tips of his boots.

Trembling with fear, Mila tried to crawl away. The others roared with laughter, but fortunately, nobody dismounted to join in the sport. After a while, the man remounted his horse and the band rode off.

When he had recovered sufficiently, Mila checked to find the treasure hidden in his waist belt, a turquoise and several gold coins, was still safe. He gave heartfelt thanks to the Deities for protecting him, and hurried out of Kampa territory.

但他們卻停下了，並逐漸向他靠近。米拉被高大的黑衣人圍着，還有醜陋、滿口泡沫的恐怖吠狗，把他嚇得虛脫了！快要暈倒了！

幫首領下命令，一個高大的騎士下馬，他用一隻手把米拉從地下揪起來，用可怕的眼神瞪着他，用力地搖他，突然把他倒轉搖晃。米拉口袋裏的小刀、梳子、硬幣和一些零星都散出來了。

那人把米拉放開，就像扔下一袋爛布裹着的骨頭。然後不斷的用靴尖去踢。米拉恐懼、顫抖，戰戰兢兢的爬行。其他人哈哈大笑，幸而沒有人下馬參與。過了不久，那人重新上馬和他的黨羽離開了。

米拉鎮定下來後，他檢查藏在腰間的綠松石和幾枚金幣，幸好都還在。他衷心的感謝諸神的保護，趕忙離開了甘巴族地區。

Chapter 6
PILGRIMAGE

After another two days' journey, Mila arrived at a point from where he could view Mount Kailas standing in splendid isolation away from the Himalayan ranges. He was awed by the round peak in bright sunlight, glowing like a huge golden dome, crowned with silvery snow. He prostrated himself in devotion. According to the Holy Texts of the Bonn Sect, the Prophet had descended from heaven in ancient times, using the snowy peak as a ladder. Mount Kailas was the dwelling place of three hundred and sixty gods. Every Tibetan man dreamed of making the pilgrimage to Mount Kailas at least once in his lifetime for, by walking around the mountain once, a devotee would be cleansed of all his sins in this life. Mila was very glad to add his stone to a huge pile of stones that had accumulated through centuries of pilgrim visits. Colourful prayer flags fluttered over them.

Mila joined the stream of pilgrims who came from all parts of Tibet, Nepal and India. Many performed the *kyancha*, kneeling down and getting up again, every step of the way. Oblivious to the glare and heat of the sun and the pelting sand storms, all bowed their heads and prayed incessantly *a-ma-ni-ba-mi-mu*. Following the Bonn tradition, Mila walked

第六章
朝聖

經過兩天的行程，米拉看到孤峯屹立，遠離喜馬拉雅山脈的神山。明亮的陽光照耀下，那圓山峰好像巨大的金頂，又蓋着如銀冠的白雲。他滿懷敬畏，俯伏祈禱，想着波恩教派的聖文，古時，先知從天上沿着天梯徐徐降臨白雪皚皚的山頂，這山峯是三百六十位神祇的居所。每個藏族男人都嚮往在一生中能有一次到神山朝聖，繞着山將一生中的罪孽得以潔淨。五個巨大的瑪尼堆是數世紀朝聖者供奉的石塊，彩色繽紛的風馬旗在空中飄揚，米拉慶幸能添加了他的石子。

米拉加入來自西藏、尼泊爾、印度的朝聖人群中。大家都實行大禮拜儀式：跪下禮拜、起來，再跪下、再起來，一再反覆的跪拜，忘卻了刺眼，酷熱的陽光，急降的沙暴，連續不斷的禱告，唸着喃嘸觀世音菩薩（嗡嘛呢白麥奉）。依着波恩教的傳統，米拉從左走到右，手裏拿着祈禱輪。佛教徒走在相反的方向，從右到左。突然有人像奔馳的馬匹，迅

around from left to right, with a prayer wheel in his hand; however, the Buddhists were walking in the opposite direction, from right to left. Suddenly, someone whisked past him, as fast as a galloping horse. This must be the mysterious Bonn rapid walking he had heard about, and resolved that he would learn to do it too. During the fifteen days of walking around the mountain, he felt peace slowly growing in his mind.

At night, Mila lodged in the small monasteries nearby, and performed his devotions with other pilgrims. Whenever he had the opportunity, he sought out Bonn worshippers and talked to them about their religion. He learned that their most respected sorcerer and teacher of black magic was Yungtun of Yarlung.

Yungtun was born with big donkey ears and, although he always wore a broad-brimmed hat to hide them, he was easily distinguishable. According to hearsay, he had been abducted by the Devil in his childhood and held captive for twelve years. When he finally returned home, he was conversant with black magic. As an adult, he was converted to Buddhism and became a Lama of the Bonn Sect, soon becoming famous with many followers.

Mila decided to beg Yungtun to be his guru and to accept him as a *chela*, a disciple, but first Mila needed to present him with valuable gifts. His mother had foreseen this necessity and had scraped together all they had to purchase the gifts – a

速的走過，他知道這就是他下決心要學習的波恩疾步。在他

繞山行走的第十五天，他感覺到心情慢慢的平靜下來。晚上

米拉寄宿在附近的小寺廟，與其他的朝聖者打成一片。一有

機會，他就會找波恩善信談論他們的宗教，得知他們最受尊

敬的巫師和黑魔法老師是雅龍村的永敦巴。

　　永敦巴長着一對大驢耳，他常戴一頂寬邊的帽子把耳朵

遮住，但他還是很容易被認出來。傳說他孩提時曾經被魔鬼

綁架，到十二歲時才被釋放。當他回家時，他已經熟悉黑魔

法。成人後，他轉奉波恩教派。不久便是成名的喇嘛，更有

許多追隨者。

　　米拉決定乞求永敦巴收他為門徒。在拜師入門時，米拉

需要送貴重的禮物。他媽媽早有準備，湊齊他們僅有的，買

了禮物——就是米拉藏在外套裏美麗的綠松石和幾枚金

beautiful turquoise and several gold coins, hidden inside his coat. However, Mila felt these material gifts were not quite sufficient, and it was more important that Yungtun be moved by his sincerity.

Mila made his way southeast, towards the Sacred Lake. The scenery was indescribably beautiful and Mount Kailas, perfectly reflected in the crystal clear water, seemed to grow out of the lake. Mila bathed in the icy water and felt its magic, believing the holy water would cleanse him of the five deadly sins and purify his heart. From the lake, he took a small stone and some holy water, going on his way with lighter steps. On his long trek, he gradually descended to the tree-line and, further down, hit the Tsangpo River. His plan was to follow the river until he reached Yarlung Village near the Nepal border, where he expected to find Yungtun, the great sorcerer.

It was well into spring and, as the weather grew much warmer, Mila had to remove his overcoat. The narrow river gorge was green with trees, vines and bushes, some of which were subtropical. He saw the broad leaves of a banana plant, monkeys and small apes swinging through the trees, and the air was filled with the cries of monkeys and birds and the buzzing of bees. Surely he was getting close to Yarlung, the well-known Paradise Village, where the mild winter temperature was never lower than minus ten degrees Celsius. He kept on walking by

幣。米拉覺得這些都不足夠，最要緊的是永敦巴會被他的真誠所感動。

米拉取道東南方，朝着聖湖走（瑪旁雍錯湖）。沿途的風景美得無與倫比，神山倒影在清澈的湖水中，仿佛要從湖中升起。米拉浸泡在冰冷的湖水中，感受到它的魔力，相信聖水能淨化他的罪過,更可以潔淨他的心靈。他從湖裏拿了一小塊石頭和一些聖水，踏着輕鬆的腳步繼續他的行程。他長途跋涉，從山頂逐漸下降到孔雀河（馬甲藏布）。他計劃沿着河邊走，直到抵達接近尼泊爾邊境的雅龍村莊，在那裏他盼望能找到偉大的魔法師—永敦巴。

大地回春，天氣暖和，米拉卸掉身上的大衣。狹谷滿是茂盛的綠樹、籐、和灌木叢。有些亞熱帶的植物，他看到寬葉的芭蕉。猴子和小猩猩正在樹叢間搖蕩，猴子和鳥的叫聲，更有蜜蜂的嗡嗡聲。他知道已逐漸接近雅龍——著名的

the clear rushing water, still icy cold, and greatly enjoying his new surroundings, so very different from his home in the harsh western highland.

Where the river gorge eventually broadened out to a green stretch of mountain pasture, hundreds of sheep, cows, horses and yaks grazed in the lush meadows against a backdrop of shining glaciers. As the herdsmen were friendly, Mila decided to stay and rest for a day or two. At night he was allowed into their tent and invited to share their food. In the daytime, he helped the women with milking and butter-making. As a reward, he was given pats of yellow butter and a small sack of dry cheese. He felt happy and rested, despite the fact that he had constantly to take care to avoid their ferocious guard dogs, kept to protect the herd from the marauding wolves and leopards. The dogs were not chained and would attack any unwary stranger who ventured too close.

The herdsmen told Mila that he was only two or three days' walk from reaching Yarlung. One fine day, he got up early in the morning, took their leave and resumed his journey.

As he followed the bank of the Tsangpo River, picking his way among the large rocks, he came suddenly face to face with a huge black bear. The bear was just as surprised as he was, for it had been fishing in the shallows and the sound of rushing water had muffled Mila's approaching footsteps. Mila, unarmed,

天堂村，那裏的天氣溫和，沒有嚴冬。他繼續沿着清澈、湍急的河行走。河水雖然還是冰冷，但他卻滿享受這新環境，這裏與他西部高山艱苦的家鄉有天淵之別。

河道逐漸擴大，伸展至一片綠油油的平原。數以百計的羊、牛、馬和犛牛在蒼翠茂盛的草地上吃草，襯托着的是閃亮冰川的背景。牧人們很友善，米拉便在這裏停留數天。晚上他就睡在帳幕裏，還可以分享他們的食物。白天他幫忙婦女們擠牛奶和製作黃油，他獲得小塊黃油和一小袋的乾乳酪作爲報酬。他感到很開心，也很舒坦。他只需要小心避開兇猛的哨狗，為了保護羊群不被狼和豹襲擊，狗是沒有鏈鎖着的，隨時會襲擊任何靠近的陌生人。牧人告訴米拉他只要步行兩三天就可以到達雅龍了。他選了一個晴朗的早晨，又恢復他的行程。

他沿着河邊，正在岩石隙間找路徑時，突然面對面的是一隻龐大的黑熊！黑熊也很驚慌，牠一直在淺水中捕魚，流水的聲音淹沒了米拉的腳步聲。米拉手無寸鐵，當場嚇得發

was frozen with fear; however, the bear just turned around and lumbered off into the bushes. Mila fell to the ground and prostrated himself, stood up and prayed, *a-ma-ni-ba-mi-mu*, and again prostrated himself. He did the *kyangcha* hundreds of times to thank the gods for sparing his life. When he had calmed down, he sat by the river and reflected on this event. He believed this incident was a very good omen and highly auspicious. Yungtun would certainly accept him and agree to be his guru. Mila went on his way cheerfully, feeling grateful.

呆了。然而黑熊卻轉身，笨重的移進灌木叢。米拉跪倒在地上，衰憊的站起來祈禱「喃嘸觀世音菩薩」，一再拜倒，他做大禮拜數以百計感謝神恩。當他平靜下來，坐在河邊反思，他相信這次的意外是非常好的預兆，永敦巴肯定會接受他為徒，米拉懷着愉快感激的心情再度踏上旅途。

Guru Yungtun
喇嘛

Chapter 7

SCHOOL OF MAGIC

As Mila emerged from the narrow mountain pass, he saw a cluster of houses nestled in the valley below. He knew immediately that this was Yarlung. Spurred on by excitement, he quickened his steps, not paying attention to the beautiful scenery. The hill slopes here were covered with green bamboo and tall red cedar trees, and he passed a forest of rhododendrons in full bloom. Soon he arrived at the village where, except for a few stone houses, most of the dwellings were built of red cedar-wood. Gardens of flowers bloomed everywhere.

A procession made its way through the narrow streets. At the front walked a man beating a kettledrum and two men blowing conch shells, followed by a band of more than twenty in colourful silk robes. In their midst, an imposing looking Lama walked under a huge yellow umbrella. Mila thought this man must be Yungtun, and followed the procession at a little distance until they stopped at a house near the river.

In the orchard, where all kinds of apple, apricot and fruit trees blossomed, a feast was laid out near a gurgling stream. The lady of the house came to the front door, dressed in silk with gold ornaments in her hair. Mila asked her for alms, saying that he was a traveler and had come a long way. She generously gave

第七章
魔法學校

當米拉從山徑穿出，他看見一列的房子坐落在山谷中。他意識到這就是雅龍了。他不顧眼前的美景，很興奮的加緊腳步。山坡長滿翠綠的竹，高聳的紅杉樹，他越過杜鵑花盛開的森林，很快已到達村莊。莊裏除了幾間石屋外，似乎所有的房屋都是紅杉木建成的。處處都是花朵綻放的庭園。

一列隊伍在狹窄的街道上遊行。領隊在敲打着鼓鈸，另外兩個人吹着螺號，跟隨着的二十多人穿着彩色綢緞長袍。在他們之中，一位莊嚴的喇嘛正走在黃色的傘下。米拉認為這人就是他要找的永敦巴。他跟隨這群人走了一小段路，直至他們停留在河邊的一所房子前。

這園子裏，各種各樣的蘋果、杏和果樹正在開花，在汩汩水聲的小溪邊已佈置了一個盛會。女主人穿着絲綢，髮上戴着金飾走到前門來。米拉向她要求佈施，說自己是從遠方來的旅者。她慷慨的給了他很多食物，還讓他坐進果園裏享用。

him a large portion of the food and allowed him to sit in the orchard to enjoy it.

The members of the procession feasted for several hours, from mid-morning to early afternoon, drinking beer, taking snuff, singing and dancing. Mila discovered that the man everybody addressed as Rimpoche was indeed Yungtun, and he was wearing a wide-brimmed hat that covered his big ears. He was in his early fifties, tall and strong, and rather stern-looking. His wife, Yanchela, was kind and elegant. By listening to the conversation, Mila learned that the feast would be followed by an initiation ceremony for new disciples, and felt extremely fortunate to have come at such an opportune time. Most of the guests left after the feast, and only a small group of disciples and members of the family remained behind. Mila boldly went into the house with them.

It was a large three-storied house, like Mila's own home, the "Four And Eight", but much finer. It was built of red cedar boards with intricately carved doorframes and window frames, painted in bright colours. The ground floor was a stable for horses and dogs. Everyone climbed a ladder to the living room on the second floor. Mila was dazzled by its magnificence. In the centre was an open fireplace for logs and on both sides were placed thick, stiff mattresses for sitting and resting, and small low tables. Brightly-coloured wooden storage chests painted with floral patterns sat against the walls.

　　盛宴從早上一直延續到下午，他們喝啤酒、吸鼻咽、唱歌及跳舞。米拉發覺被人尊稱為「仁波切」的喇嘛，果然是永敦巴！他戴了一項寬邊的帽子遮住大耳朵。大約是五十歲，高個子，強壯，樣子有點嚴厲。他的太太賢切拉很和藹，高貴。從他們的談話中，米拉得知宴會後將會有一個收新徒弟儀式，他很慶幸有這難得的機緣。宴會後大部分的賓客都離開，只有徒弟和家人還留下。米拉鼓起勇氣跟着眾人走進房子裏。

　　那是一座三層的樓房，像米拉的家一樣，但這房子較為精緻。紅杉木窗框和門框刻着圖案又漆上顏色。樓下是個大牲口柵。要爬上樓梯才能進入居室。華麗的大廳令米拉目不暇給。廳的中間是燒柴的爐，兩邊放置着厚而硬的坐墊和低矮的桌子，墙邊的木櫃繪有色彩鮮豔的花卉。

However, this was primarily a place of worship. It had a beautifully carved wooden altar that held burning butter lamps in front of an enormous Thangka, which hung from ceiling to floor.

The Black God of Bonn, embroidered on the Thangka, had black eyeballs staring from red sockets in a large black face, a crown of human skulls and a magnificent robe. Surrounding him was a depiction of the beginning of the world. Two rays of light shone from the void where two eggs came into being, one black and one white. The White God came from the white egg and the Black God from the other. The Black God married the pure, kind Goddess of the Lakes, sewn in blue and silver, and she gave birth to eighteen brothers and sisters. These minor deities eventually populated the world.

Yungtun and his wife sat on the mattresses on each side of the altar. Standing behind Yungtun was his head disciple, Darma, a powerful-looking young man. Everyone else crowded near the entrance, sitting on the floor. A couple from a neighbouring farm came forward first, leading their eight-year-old twin daughters. The father said, "Oh Reverend Master, we give you our daughters to be your handmaidens. Please enlighten their minds and make them soothsayers. We also present to you a flock of sheep and a fine pair of yaks that can produce young ones. Please accept our gifts." As Yungtun knew the neighbours very

　　這裏是拜神的地方，有一個精美彫花木製的聖壇，壇上燃燒着酥油燈，巨大的「唐卡」從天花垂到地面。

　　唐卡的刺繡畫的主題就是<u>波恩教</u>的傳說。<u>波恩</u>黑神有一張大黑臉，一對黑眼球從紅色的眼眶裏凝視着，頭戴着骷髏皇冠，穿着華麗的長袍。圍着他的是一幅幅畫，描敘盤古初開的的世界。兩道光在空間照着即將孵化的兩隻蛋，一黑一白。白神從白蛋裏出來，黑神從另外的黑蛋出來。黑神與純潔，善良的湖泊女神結婚，她穿着藍和銀色的袍。她又生下十八個子女，這些諸神的後代逐漸填滿了整個世界。

　　<u>永敦巴</u>和他的妻子坐在聖壇兩邊的墊子上。站在後邊的是他的首徒，<u>達爾瑪</u>是一個健壯的青年。大家都擠在近大門口的地下坐着。第一對夫妻走上前，他們就是從鄰近農莊來的，帶着一對孿生姐妹。爸爸說：「尊貴的<u>仁波切</u>，我們的兩個女兒送給您當小婢！請您啓發她們，使她們能夠占卜。我們還送上一群羊和一對可以生育的好犛牛。請接受我們的禮物吧！」<u>永敦巴</u>和他們素有往來，欣然同意收女孩子為

well, he readily agreed to train the girls. They would be able to practise soothsaying until they turned fifteen, and then they would be ready to wed, losing their magical powers after marriage.

An exceedingly tall, well-built young man with a shiny black face, attended by two servants, knelt before Yungtun. His name was Norbu and he belonged to the Kongba tribe. His hair was braided and he wore rich clothing decorated with coral necklaces and a heavily-jewelled belt. He said, "Reverend Master, please accept my horse. It is a rare breed, swift as the wind, fitted with a precious saddle that is soft and comfortable and richly decorated with jewels and gold. This horse was my pride, and now I give it to you to ride."

Yungtun answered, "I have a gallant steed driven by my breath and I gallop to the four corners of the world at will. I do not need your horse."

Norbu thought that Yungtun considered his gift of a horse too meagre and that this was why he refused it. Instead, he removed a piece of luminous green jade from his belt and presented it saying, "To prove that I am no miser, this is my father's most precious legacy. Reverend Master, it goes without saying that I, and all I have, belong to you. In return for this offering, I beg you to initiate me and teach me what you know of black magic, and give me the texts."

徒。她們占卜靈驗直到十五歲，到時她們會出嫁，婚後她們的法力就會消失。

一個高大、魁梧、臉有光澤的年輕人，帶着兩個僕人來到永敦巴面前。他的名字叫那博，是康巴族人，他的頭髮編成大辮子，穿戴華麗，有珊瑚項鏈和寶石腰帶。他說：「敬愛的仁波切，請收下我的馬，牠是稀有的千里馬，疾如風，又裝上寶石和金子裝飾的軟馬鞍。這是我引以為傲的馬匹，我奉獻給您，做您的坐騎。」

永敦巴回答說：「我已能驅使我的駿馬，奔馳到世界的任何角落。我不需要你的馬！」

那博以爲他的禮物太微薄了，所以被拒絕。於是他從腰間拿下一枚通透漂亮的綠玉，説道：「您看我不是一個守財奴！這是我父親給我最珍貴的遺物。您是我的主人！不消說，您擁有我本身和我所有的財物，只求您教我您精通的黑魔法，和給我傳授經文。」

"I have some of the most potent mantras and very rare scriptures," Yungtun said, "but to impart such truths has very strict conditions attached. You must promise to obey me absolutely in everything."

Norbu promised faithfully to obey and then he was initiated.

Two brothers, Lhoba hunters, came from the eastern forests carrying long-bows and arrows on their backs. They had a letter of recommendation from their father who was also a Bonn Lama and a friend of Yungtun. They, too, carried valuable gifts, including a tiger skin and some leopard pelts. Yanchela was particularly pleased to see the brothers and enquired after their mother. They also received their initiation.

Yungtun suddenly turned his head and pointed at Mila, asking, "Who do we have here?"

Mila knelt down. "Most Reverend Master, you are renowned throughout the land. I am Mila Thopaga from the village of Kyanga-Tsa, and I have come a long way to seek your instruction. My uncle and aunt have deprived me of my entire fortune, making my mother and sister destitute. My mother has ordered me to learn black magic so that we can punish them. Please accept this beautiful turquoise and five gold pieces, which is all that we have. I offer you my life and my body in return for instruction in your art."

「我有非常罕有的經典和厲害的咒語，」永敦巴說：「但我傳授這魔法是有條件的，就是你要答應絕對服從我。」

那博誠懇的答應服從，於是他被接納了。

兩兄弟是珞巴族獵人，背着弓箭，來自東方的森林。他們有父親的推薦書。 他們的父親是永敦巴的朋友，也是波恩喇嘛。他們亦獻上貴重的禮物，包括虎皮和豹皮。賢切拉很開心見到他們，還問候他們的母親。當然他們被接納了。

永敦巴突然轉過頭，指着米拉，問道：「他是誰啊？」

米拉跪了下來：「尊貴的仁波切，我是米拉特巴加，來自貢唐村。我長途跋涉來這裏求您收我為徒。我的伯父和姑媽強奪了我們全家的財產，使我媽媽和妹妹無以為生。於是我媽媽命我學會黑魔法以懲罰他們。請您收下這塊綠松石和五枚金幣，這些是我家所有的一切。我奉獻給您我的身體和性命來報答您的傳授。」

Yungtun smiled and said, "I will consider your request." After some thought, he decided to accept Mila and instruct him as he requested. Mila was overjoyed when he was also initiated and allowed to stay.

Yungtun sang this benediction before the congregation dispersed:

You faithful disciples who have travelled far to come here,
In return for your reverence, I shall expound to you the Holy Doctrine.
Do you intend to practise the Holy Doctrine with all your soul?
Do you earnestly practise the Holy Doctrine with all your heart?
Has Faith been born in the depth of your being?
There is no end to the deeds that may be done,
In whatsoever pleases you,
If you practise the Holy Doctrine!

永敦巴微笑着說：「我會考慮你的請求。」經過考慮後，

他決定收米拉為徒，米拉欣喜若狂得知被接納入門。

永敦巴在散會前唱祝福誦：

忠誠的門徒，感謝你們遠道而來，
我會向你們把教義詳細講解，
你是否決心學習這些神聖的教義？
你會不會全心去實行這神聖的教義？
在你的心靈深處是否有信仰？
只要你能奉行這些神聖的教義，
世上無難事，一切都會如你所願！

Chapter 8
PLAGUE

Mila found that his life as a disciple in Yungtun's large household was quite congenial. He lived in a small hut by himself, away from the house and near the fields. He rose at dawn each day to take care of the animals or work in the fields, and then he joined the household for a meal at mid-morning. After eating this meal, Yungtun instructed the disciples in a study program that prepared them to become a Lama when they returned home. They were taught different sacrificial rites: to bless a house or the fields; to ward off evil or bad luck; to make rain; to curse an enemy; and the important skill of healing the sick.

Mila got on well with his peers, especially the two brothers from the Lhoba forests who initiated him into the forbidden pleasure of hunting. In most parts of the country, hunting was not allowed, as the taking of animal life was considered sinful.

Yungtun gave his neighbours' little girls special training in soothsaying. They learned to tell fortunes by gazing into a brass mirror, or even at their own fingernails. As they had the power of telepathy between them, when they joined forces, their ability to penetrate into the future was formidable. Sometimes they stayed overnight with Yanchela, but more often they went home

第八章
瘟疫

在永敦巴的大家庭裏，米拉在門徒中過着融洽的日子。米拉

有自己的小屋，靠近田地。他每天黎明起床，照顧動物或在

田裏工作。隨後大夥兒一起吃早餐。餐後，永敦巴給門徒上

課，訓練他們成為專業的喇嘛。課程包括不同的祭祀：祝福

房子或田地、抵禦邪惡、造雨、詛咒敵人，最重要的是醫治

病患。米拉和同輩們相處得不錯，他特別喜歡珞巴森林來的

兩兄弟。他們帶領他去打獵，而打獵是被禁止的活動，因為

獵殺動物被認爲是罪惡的行爲。

永敦巴傳授占卜術給鄰居的兩個女孩。她們算命時是只

靠注視着一面銅鏡，或者是她們自己的指甲。這對孿生姐妹

能心靈相通，所以當她們聯合起來就極之靈驗。她倆有時候

會留校過夜，但大多數都在下午騎騾子由米拉送回家。米拉

to their parents in the afternoon. They both rode on a donkey that Mila led on foot, bringing the animal home afterwards. He liked to talk and joke with them on the way, for their rosy cheeks and bright laughter reminded him of Peta, his younger sister. On many occasions he was invited to an enjoyable dinner at their farm.

It was well into autumn, and the stars were disappearing in the night sky, when the village was stricken by an epidemic. This was a serious threat, for it was unclear whether the many symptoms indicated only one disease, or several such as typhoid, dysentery, and influenza, and already there was a heavy death toll of both people and animals. Yungtun was kept busy giving consultations to the sick, while the disciples helped by preparing and dispensing the medicine. Yungtun often took time to gather healing herbs from the mountain, accompanied by Darma.

As the twins had not come to school for several days, Mila was sent to visit them. When he arrived at the farm, he found that it was unusually quiet. The dogs were lying dead in the stable on the ground floor, and when he went up the ladder to the living room, he found that all the servants had fled. The farmer and his wife were bedridden, while the twins were delirious with fever, their rosy cheeks pale and their bodies wasted. Mila boiled some water for them to drink and tried his best to make them more comfortable. He was reluctant to leave

常常一路和她們談笑，女孩的蘋果臉和清脆的笑聲使他想起他的小妹妹百德。有時她們的父母也會邀請米拉同進晚餐。

已是晚秋，月暗星沉的黑夜，可怕的流行病肆虐在村裏。這情況引起恐慌，尤其是有很多病狀出現，但起因不明。到底是一種病或是幾種呢？如痢疾、傷寒，流行性感冒等。死亡的人和動物的數字日漸增加。永敦巴每天都忙於醫病，徒弟們就幫忙製藥和派發藥物。永敦巴常常由徒弟陪着上山採草藥做補給。

小姐妹已經幾天沒有上學了。米拉被派到農場去探訪。他發現農場是出奇的靜默！幾只狗好像臥死在馬廄裏。當他走上樓梯到屋裏，發現僕人都逃跑了，農人和他的妻子臥床不起。兩女孩子的粉紅臉變得很蒼白，身體消瘦，在神志不清地胡言亂語。米拉煮了些開水給他們喝，竭力讓他們覺得舒適。米拉不得離開他們，幸好永敦巴隨着到來又帶了藥

them, but fortunately Yungtun followed him to the farm and brought medicine. Mila brewed medicinal tea for them to drink, and Yungtun performed the purification rite by burning incense sticks and chanting mantras. Mila was relieved to see the family resting more comfortably.

It was already late afternoon when Yungtun and Mila left the farm. Yungtun thought that the girls were out of danger, but he wanted to go and gather more herbs and asked Mila to accompany him. After climbing halfway up the mountain, they came to a lush green pasture where all kinds of fragrant herbs grew, and a crystal-clear stream meandered through banks of wild flowers. In the few hours of daylight left, they gathered as much as possible, and when night fell, they prepared to make their way home in the clear moonlight.

Suddenly, in the dusk, a radiantly beautiful lady approached them. She was elegantly dressed; her white silk robe was embroidered with a pattern of flowers and red flames, her skirt was edged with pearls and beads, and sparkling diamonds circled her neck and waist.

She said, "Oh Rimpoche, my big sister, Shendormo, is very ill. Will you please come and help her? She lives on the mountain across from here."

"It's late already," Yungtun answered. "We can all stay here and I will go with you when it's daylight."

物。米拉煮了藥讓他們喝下，永敦巴又行淨化儀式；焚香和唸咒語。米拉看到這一家子都比較舒適，他就安心了。

在下午永敦巴和米拉離開農場時，永敦巴認爲女孩們已經脫離危險了，他請米拉陪他上山多採一些草藥。他們爬上半山，到達一片蒼翠繁茂的草原，長滿了各種芬芳的草藥。一條清澈的小溪，流過大片的野花。天要黑了，他們得盡快採藥。當夜幕低垂時，他們在月光照耀下穩步回家。

突然從黑暗中，一位艷光四射的女郎走出來。她穿着白絲袍繡着花朵和紅色火焰，裙邊瓖了珍珠，閃亮的鑽石圍繞着頸項和纖腰。

她說：「仁波切啊！我的大姐沈地母病得很厲害，請你幫忙醫治她吧！她就住在對面的山上。」

「現在已經很晚了，」永敦巴答道：「我們不如留在這裏等到天亮時再去。」

The lady was very insistent. "I know the way and it's not difficult at all. Please do come immediately!"

Yungtun frowned. "I really don't see how we can get there in the dark, but if you lead the way, we'll follow."

The lady took a white silk hada[3] from under her sleeve and threw it into the air, saying, "This will take us there easily." They followed her on to the hada. In a flash, it flew across the valley and they arrived at the mountain retreat.

A pure white silk tent with a door curtain of gold cloth had been pitched on the snowy ledge. When they entered, Mila was dazzled by the incredible opulence he saw; the ropes were strung with gems of different colours, each nail was marked with a head of jade, and the central pillar was inlaid with mother-of-pearl. A beautiful lady reclined on a couch at the centre, her long black hair braided with pearls, but her face was very pale. She trembled, staring with flaming eyes, and struggled to half-raise herself. "Rimpoche," she pleaded, "I am seriously ill. Please help me."

Yungtun asked, "How do you feel, and how long have you been ill? Do you know the cause?"

"This summer, the shepherd boys started a huge mountain fire that burned for ten days. I was affected by the fumes and smoke and felt sick immediately," Shendormo said. "By autumn, I was much worse. In the last few days, it has become

那女士非常堅持：「我認識路，一點都沒有問題，請立即隨我去吧！」

永敦巴皺着眉頭說：「我真不明白，天那麼黑我們要怎麼去呢！不過如果你帶路，我們就跟着吧！」

女郎從袖子裏拿出一條白絲巾來向空中拋去，說道：「很容易的！這絲巾就會帶我們過去。」他們跟着她上了絲巾，一掠而過，飛越過山谷，已到達山上隱密的居所。

雪地上有一個純白色絲帳篷，安着黃金布的門簾。當他們進入帳篷內，豪華的裝飾，使米拉驚羨不已；繩子串着不同顏色的寶石，翡翠的釘子頭，柱子鑲嵌着珍珠母。當中一個美女躺在睡椅上，她烏溜溜的長辮子編着珍珠，但她的臉卻非常蒼白。她在顫抖，眼睛發紅，掙扎着提起她的身子。

「仁波切，」她懇求着，「我病得很厲害，請幫我啊！」

永敦巴問道：「你覺得怎樣了？你病了多久？你知道起因嗎？」

「今年夏季牧童們燒山火，燒了十天。我被煙霧薰到立即感到不適，接着病了。」沈地母說道。「到了秋季，我病得更厲害。過去幾天我實在覺得無法忍受。我呼出的病毒正在傳染其他的人。我真的需要您的幫助。」

unbearable. I am so sick that my contaminated breath is spreading the infectious disease to the people. I really need your help."

Yungtun realised that she was a powerful spirit, and the cause of the plague, and he could not help her lightly. She would have to swear not to cause harm to others. "Lady, you have so much understanding and wisdom in your soul, yet you are causing injuries to others. You are laden with sin!"

She bowed her head. "I am a disciple of Padma-tod-prin. I heard the words of truth from him long ago. Although I have a great longing for the Holy Religion, I chose to nourish this evil body and satisfy my hunger as I rove through the villages. When I saw gifted ones with the capacity for dharma, I showed them the way of truth and helped them to do good deeds.

"Yet still I enjoyed eating flesh and blood! I lusted after tall, handsome men and entered their souls; as for beautiful women, in all of them I stimulated their desire, and then watched and enjoyed their passionate embrace. With my mind, I have even provoked conflict between nations. Rimpoche, I am in such misery because I cannot abstain from such terrible sins!"

永敦巴知道她是有法力的仙女，也是瘟疫傳播的源頭，絕不能輕易地幫她。他要她起誓不能再傷害他人：「小姐，你的靈魂充滿智慧和念力，但你卻運用來傷害人，你真是充滿罪惡！」

她低下頭，「我是蓮花生大師的徒弟，很久以前他已教我真理，雖然我渴望神聖的宗教，但當我在各村莊遊蕩時，我還是會選擇了滋養這邪惡的身體和滿足我的慾望。不過當我遇上那些有慧根的人，我會向他們說出真理，幫助他們向善。」

「但我仍然享受吃血和肉！我貪戀高而帥的男人，會進入他們的靈魂裏。那些漂亮的女人，我會刺激她們的慾望，然後觀看和享受我惡作劇的結果。我甚至挑起國家之間的衝突，引起戰爭。仁波切，我很痛苦又無能力自拔，我多麼想摒棄這可怕的罪行！」

Deeply moved by her confession, Yungtun chanted this to her:

You fair daughter of the Gods,
Lend me your ears and awaken your mind!
The frolics of goddesses though merry, soon fade away.
What brings great enjoyment leads to perdition!
Consider the sufferings you have brought to the beings of the
world,
And when it is considered, let your heart be moved!

Consider that in your previous life, you were a world being,
And then let your intentions be good, for the benefit of mankind!
Meditate upon the uncertainty of the hour of death.
Unless you think clearly on what causes every good or evil deed,
You will suffer the unbearable miseries of hell,
Surpassing by far your present sufferings!

"I cannot sympathise with you," Yungtun then told her, "as your present suffering is what you deserve". You know the Holy Doctrine's teachings on cause and effect, yet you have ignored it. Instead of patiently bearing a little pain and suffering, you have caused death and injury to many people. Unless you swear to stop the plague, I cannot help you!"

When she saw him get up to leave, she frantically grabbed his coat and said, "Forgive me, Rimpoche! I have been ignorant and foolish, and it was never my intention to harm people, or cause the plague. When a fire destroyed the homes of my

<u>永敦巴</u>已被她的懺悔所感動，對她唱出：

啊，美麗女神！請聽我言來喚醒你的心，
仙女們的嬉笑玩樂，很快就會過去，
那些極大的歡樂會令人步向毀滅。

試想，你帶給世人的痛苦！當你考慮到這點時，
願你的心會被感動，會改變！
細想你的前生，你也曾是人類的一分子，
你要有好的意圖，有益於人。

你要經常冥想死亡隨時會降臨！
除非你能清楚善惡形成的主因，
你將會遭受地獄的無窮苦難。
遠遠超越你目前所受的痛苦！

「我不同情你，」<u>永敦巴</u>告訴她，「目前你所受的痛苦是你

罪有應得。你明知因果的教義，然而你卻忽視祂。你不能忍

受小小的痛苦，卻令許多人受傷和死亡。除非你停止這場瘟

疫，否則我不會幫你的！」

當她看見他起身要離開時，她發狂的抓着他的上衣，説

道：「請原諒我的無知和愚昧，<u>仁波切</u>，我從來沒有打算去

傷害人，或導致瘟疫。當火災燒毀了我許多親戚的家，成千

129

relatives, thousands of demons, yaksas (ghosts) and flesh-eating sisters emerged. They have done most of the harm – they like flesh and blood, and have caused the heavy death toll. I swear to obey you and help the villagers to get well. Please don't desert me now!"

Yungtun relented and performed the purification rite for her, and then he and Mila kept up a vigil of prayer the whole night through. By the next morning, she was well enough to sit up in bed and join in the prayer. They prayed devoutly for seven days. By then she was completely well, even radiant with health and beauty.

Yungtun said, "Lady, now that you have recovered, I must go to the sick villagers immediately. Please tell me what to do, what rites and sacrifices would be effective to rid them of this plague."

"We spirits of the land and the villagers are mutually dependent," Shendormo said. "If we are well and happy, then they are also well and prosperous. Their flocks multiply and their fields produce good crops. However, even if one of the Dakinis[4] is injured, the rest of us will come to her support. Consequently there will be great turmoil in the whole environment."

She advised Yungtun what should take place: public worshipping in each village; people to join in praying, reading

上萬的惡魔、鬼怪和貪婪血肉的姐妹們走了出來，到處遊蕩。他們給人類帶來巨大的災害。我發誓服從您和幫助治好村民，請您現在不要離棄我！」

永敦巴終於緩和下來，替她行了潔淨儀式。他和米拉通宵禱告守護，第二天早晨，她已經可以坐起來，並參加祈禱。大家虔誠的禱告了七天，然後她完全痊癒了，恢復了往昔的容光煥發和美貌。

永敦巴說：「小姐，現在你已復原了，我要立即趕回到患病的村民。請你告訴我要怎麼做，用什麼儀式和犧牲才能有效地消除這場瘟疫。」

「我們地仙和村民息息相關，」沈地母說：「當我們健康和快樂的時候，他們也健康繁榮。他們的牲口加倍繁殖，田裏豐收。然而只要一個精靈受傷，其他精靈都會支持他，於是，一場大風暴就會降臨了。」

她建議永敦巴採取以下的步驟：每個村莊舉行公眾崇拜，讓村民參加祈禱、讀聖經、用聖水淨化。供奉的祭品要

of the Holy Scripture and using holy water for purification; sacrificial offerings should be plentiful, food well-cooked and decorated, with fruits of different colours. She added that alms should be given generously to the poor, and that travelling between villages should be prohibited within this period. She promised that by so doing, the plague would soon come to an end.

Yungtun and Mila walked to the nearest town, where Yungtun said to the villagers, "I had a dream which explained the cause of the epidemic to me. Not long ago, some of you started a mountain fire that injured the local Goddess. She suffered, therefore all the Dakinis and spirits became angry and caused this disease. If you perform the rites and sacrifice as I say, all will soon be well."

Following his advice, a festival of worship was held in the villages. They prayed to the three supreme Buddhas, offered sacrifice to the Guardians of the Faith, and asked for blessings on all the Dakinis and spirits. Sure enough, the terrible disease soon disappeared from the land.

充足，食物要煮熟和裝飾好，要有不同顏色的水果。賑濟窮人要慷慨，在這期間禁止外人進村莊。只要做妥這些事情，她承諾瘟疫會很快解除的。

　　永敦巴和米拉走到最近的市鎮，永敦巴告訴村民說：「我發了一個夢，夢中解釋瘟疫的成因。不久前你們有些人燒山火傷害了本地的女神。她的痛苦使所有的飛仙和精靈都很生氣，所以形成這次的災難。如果你們按照我說的舉行儀式和祭奠，情況很快會好轉的。」

　　遵循他的忠告，村莊裏舉行了崇拜日，他們向如來三寶佛祈禱，奉獻祭品給監護神，求降祝福於所有的地仙和精靈。可怕的瘟疫果然在這片土地上消失了。

Chapter 9

MONKEY DEMONS

Mila returned to his hut at sundown after a busy day working in the fields. He was carrying an armful of firewood, which he dropped in astonishment upon entering his room. Five creatures already occupied the hut. They looked like large, iron-coloured monkeys, covered in short fur, with long tails and enormous eyes. One was sitting on Mila's bed with an open book on his knees, as if reading aloud. Standing next to him was another, attentively turning the pages. Two were listening, sitting on the floor. The fifth one stood near the door, like a servant.

Mila thought, Am I delirious? After the initial shock, he managed to compose himself a little. He decided these must be spirits of the surrounding hills and household. They are offended because I have not yet paid my respects by giving them food offerings. I shall sing to them a song of praise!

Mila sang this song:

> *Oh, this valley is so peaceful,*
> *The blessed dwelling place of my Lama!*
> *High above the mountains*
> *White clouds float by,*
> *Below, the river gently flows.*
> *Tree branches are dancing in the wind,*
> *Bushes of many kinds are flowering,*
> *The air is filled with fragrance.*

第九章
猴妖

米拉整天在田裏幹活，日落時分回到茅舍。他推開大門時還抱着一梱柴。他大吃了一驚，把柴都丟下地。屋子裏有五隻類似大猴子的怪物：鐵色、短毛、長尾巴、巨大眼睛。其中一隻盤腿坐在床上，把書放在膝上，好像在大聲的唸着。另一隻站在牠旁邊仔細的翻頁。有兩隻坐在地上聽。還有一隻靠門邊站，好像是僕人。

米拉懷疑自己神志不清，他設法平靜下來。想到這些可能是附近山野的精靈，一定是因為他忘了祭奠而觸怒了牠們！他要為牠們唱一首讚美的歌，米拉抒揚地唱出：

啊，這平靜的山谷，
我喇嘛居住的福地！
白雲在山頂飄過，
潺潺溪水在地上流，
樹枝在風中跳舞，
各種叢木正綻放花朵，
空氣中滿是芬芳，

> *Bees are buzzing, birds twittering;*
> *Little birds practise flying;*
> *Little horses practise running;*
> *Mila practises learning.*
> *Oh, friendly Spirits, hear my song*
> *And return to your own places!*

The creatures were not at all appeased by Mila's song. They became even more belligerent, staring at him angrily and chattering among themselves. Two of them came near Mila and menaced him, exposing their fangs, but they kept their claws behind their backs. Mila then realised that they were demons and had come intending to do him some mischief. He tried to exorcise them by fiercely chanting incantations and commanding them loudly to depart. The demons all stood up and stamped around. Some said violent words, and others laughed, but they would not go away.

Mila was so frustrated that tears welled up in his eyes, and then he thought of *dharma*, the power of compassion. Demons were born in evil bodies as retribution for deeds of killing in their previous life. They had to nourish their bodies through doing more evil, causing harm and injury to the others, and thus they sank even lower in the Wheel of Transmigration. Mila decided to direct his mind instead to compassion and sympathy for the demons. They are, after all, he thought, sentient beings with light in their souls and, as they were reading when I came

蜜蜂嗡嗡聲，鳥兒吱吱叫，
幼鳥在學飛，幼馬在學跑，
米拉也在此學習。
友善的精靈啊，聽我的歌，
請您們快快回家！

米拉的歌並不能緩和這些妖魔，反而挑起牠們的敵意。牠們怒視米拉，又不斷的交頭接耳。有兩隻走近，露出鋒利的齒去嚇米拉，幸而牠們把手爪放在背後。米拉知道這些妖魔意圖傷害他，就大聲唸咒語去驅趕牠們，又命令他們離去。妖魔都站起，來回地跺腳。有些說話恐嚇，有些在譏笑，卻都不想離去。

米拉覺得非常困擾，忍不住要落淚了。他靈機一觸，突然悟到佛法的慈悲心！生為妖魔就是牠們前世殺生的懲罰。牠們必須不斷傷害他人，以惡行來滋養自己的肉身，因此牠們會再世沉淪。米拉決意以同情和憐憫心來開導牠們。這些妖魔也有靈性，也能被感動。當米拉進屋子時，牠們正

in, must have respect for good words. So I will preach to them.

Mila gave this sermon:

Oh, lowly creatures listen carefully!
To be born in an evil body is the retribution for deeds of killing.
To satisfy your hunger, you do evil deeds to harm others.
Sneering at me, that is your constant business,
I am not afraid of you causing me distraction!
Think of the punishments of the Wheel of Transmigration,
Renounce your evil deeds completely and
Through the efficacy of prayer, make a firm resolution.
Restrain the malice of your thoughts,
Please do not harm me.
Return again to your own place,
Oh you demons!

The demons were outraged. They gathered together in an angry throng and glared at Mila, and looked as if they were about to pounce and engulf him. Mila was desperately frightened and wanted to escape, but he suddenly remembered his Lama's teaching. His Lama said that he must keep his mind empty of fear, for demons would arise out of this terror. Mila realised that his mistake was to treat the demons as if they were outside, and not within, his mind. His courage rose and he sang this song:

Like an eagle flying in the sky,
Although the sky is wide and the earth's valleys deep below,
I do not fear!
For a flying eagle never falls from the sky.

Like a fish swimming in the sea,

在看書，明顯地牠們也重視真理。米拉開始說教：

> 低等的傢伙啊，留心聽我言！
> 生於惡身，就是你們前世殺戮的報應。
> 為了滿足飢渴，你們便為惡害人。
> 你們不斷譏笑我，
> 我不怕！你們不能使我分心。
> 想到輪迴的刑罰，你們就要真心悔改！
> 依靠禱告的力量來痛下決心，
> 永不再有惡念！
> 魔鬼啊，請不要害我，
> 你們快快回家吧！

羣魔被激得大怒！他們蜂擁而起，怒目注視米拉，像要

衝過來吞沒他！米拉被嚇壞了，想不顧一切的逃走。突然他

記起他喇嘛的教誨！喇嘛說：「人的心裏不能有恐懼，因為

心中的恐懼會產生妖魔。」米拉立刻意識到他的錯誤：他正

努力抵抗外來的妖魔，而這些妖魔卻生自他的內心！他鼓起

勇氣唱道：

> 一隻鷹在天空飛翔，
> 天空雖然廣闊，地下又是深谷，
> 我不怕！
> 飛翔的鷹肯定不會從天上掉下來。
>
> 魚兒在海裏暢游，

Although the waves are great, the nets and iron hooks many,
I do not fear!
For a fish wandering in water never drowns.

The paws of a snow lion are never frozen,
A stone cannot break a block of iron.
I, Mila, son of Darsing-kar-mo,
Practise learning and serve the Lama.
Although the demons are violent and many,
I do not fear!

Mila faced them cordially, as if they were his guests. "Sons of Pinayaya, that you came here is wonderful! Don't hurry away. Stay with me at least for tonight, and we can have a long discussion. Let's compete to see who is greater: the Black or the White Dharma. Your purpose here is obviously to obstruct my mind; you must swear not to come here again if you fail. But if you stay after losing this contest, then shame on you!"

Mila felt his heart swell with courage and pride, and he boldly charged at the demons, who became breathless and terrified. They looked timidly at each other, trembling, wavering to and fro like candle flames. Gradually, they merged into one, and then turned into a black whirlwind that rushed out of the room. After a while, Mila calmed down and realised that he had passed an important trial towards his spiritual advancement, and gained much self knowledge. The demons had come to haunt him because he had asked for black magic. However, in his

> 浪雖然大，魚網和釣鈎雖然多，
> 我不怕！
> 海中游的魚兒永不會被淹死。
>
> 雪獅的爪永不會被凍僵，
> 石頭是不能打爛鐵塊的，
> 我，米拉，大成嘉母之子，
> 尊從我的喇嘛，正在學習，
> 面對眾多兇惡的妖魔，
> 我不害怕！

米拉親切的面對牠們，好像對待客人似的：「邊那艾艾的兒子，你來這裏極好！不要急着走，至少今晚留下來。我們可以有長時間討論，讓我們來分辯，比較黑魔法和白魔法的優劣，一定要分出高低！你們到這裏來明顯的要使我分心，發誓如果你們輸了，就永不再找我！但如果輸了，你們仍然留下來，那我會極鄙視你們！」

米拉感到勇氣和自豪在心裏膨脹，他大膽的衝向羣魔，嚇得他們透不過氣來。他們膽怯地交換眼色，顫抖着像擺動的蠟燭火焰。漸漸的他們合併起來，化成一股黑旋風，衝出門外，消失在黑夜裏。過了一會米拉才平靜下來，他知道他已通過重要的考驗，而他的靈悟也晉升了，他現在更了解自己的內心。妖魔來侵犯他，是因為他正在尋求黑魔法，雖然他的內心是屬於白魔法。幸而他有足夠的勇氣去驅魔！黑魔

heart, he belonged to White Karma and he had been brave enough to repel the demons, realising that both they and the blackness originated in his own mind.

法，雖然他的內心是屬於<u>白魔法</u>。幸而他有足夠的勇氣去驅

魔！他深深領悟到：<u>黑魔法</u>和<u>白魔法</u>的起源，都是由自己的

內心產生的。

Chapter 10

GRADUATION AND SCHOOL LEAVING

During the year that Mila studied with Yungtun, his life was rather free and easy. He made friends with the other disciples, especially the Lhoba brothers. They spent their leisure time roaming the mountains, their excursions extending further and further. Their greatest pleasure was a hot spring that they had found in a bamboo forest some distance from the village. The hot water bubbled out of the ground and flowed into a rock basin on the bank of an icy stream. They enjoyed plunging alternatively into the hot pool and then the icy water.

Before the cold weather set in, Mila also went hunting with the brothers on the hills at night. As hunting was forbidden, these expeditions were particularly exciting, although mostly unsuccessful. They ran, tracking deer in the cold night air and once the brothers shot a small deer with their arrows. Mila was shocked at the taking of life, but he helped to hold down the struggling deer while his friends killed it with their knives. They brought the meat home, and enjoyed it with the other disciples the following night, feasting in secret, roasting the meat in the open air and drinking beer.

Mila saved part of the deer for himself, the head and the intestines, for a private sacrificial rite. He went to the hillside to

第十章
畢業及離校

米拉在永敦巴門下學習己經年，日子過得輕鬆愉快，他在同輩中交到不少朋友，洛巴族的兩兄弟尤其是他的好友。他們有空便一起爬山，越走越遠，令他們最感開心的事，就是在村莊附近的竹林裏找到了溫泉！暖水冒着泡從地底湧出來，流入石坑裏，一旁是冰冷的小溪，他們最大的樂趣就是來回浸泡在冷和熱水中。

在寒冬來臨之前，三人經常夜裏上山打獵。雖然沒有收穫，他們還是覺得很刺激，因為獵獸是被禁止的。他們在冷空氣中奔跑，跟蹤鹿的蹤影，只有一次，兩兄弟射中了小鹿。殺生令米拉覺得震驚，但他還是幫忙按下掙扎的鹿，讓他的朋友用刀殺死牠。他們把肉帶回家，直至第二天晚上，所有門徒都來分享鹿肉。這是一個秘密的晚會，他們在空地裏烤肉、喝啤酒。

米拉留下一些鹿肉、頭和腸子，用來做私人的獻祭。他

cut some thorny branches, which he used to fence off a triangular piece of ground. He placed the head at the centre on a pile of stones and encircled it with the bloody intestines. He then chanted and danced to the guardian gods, praying for their blessings on himself and his family and, in particular, for their help in his pursuit of black magic.

However, Mila was quite disappointed with his daily studies. He and the other disciples were learning some magic lore: an elegant rite to join heaven and earth, curses that could cause the death of an enemy, prayers and chants for the gods' blessings, and so forth. But Mila felt he was not advancing in his skills, or learning the kind of magic he needed to learn.

Mila's friends, also dissatisfied, were thinking of returning home. Norbu, a young Chief of the Kongba tribe, said to Mila, "I have learned enough. The Lama himself said that he had no more to teach. We must depend on our own application and perseverance for further development of the art. Why don't you come home with me and join our trading caravan? I'd like you to be my brother!"

Mila was tempted by the offer, for he knew that the Kongba tribe controlled some rich trading routes to China. However, he had to refuse for the sake of his mother. She would certainly kill herself, as she had threatened, if he abandoned his ambition to learn black magic and ran away to join a trading caravan.

在山邊砍了些帶刺的樹枝，用作柵欄圍出一塊三角形的地。

他把鹿頭放在當中的一堆石頭上，用血淋淋的腸子圍繞，然

後他跳舞歌頌，祈求監護神的祝福及庇佑他的家人，尤其是

要幫他學到黑魔法！

米拉對於每天的學習其實感到相當失望，他們只是學些

魔法知識包括：連接天與地的優雅儀式，詛咒敵人死亡，歌

頌神以祈求祝福等等。米拉覺得毫無進展，因為這些都不是

他所需要的。

其他門徒也頗為不滿意，想回家。年輕的康巴族酋長對

米拉說：「我學夠了，況且喇嘛也說他再沒有什麼可教我們

了。我們現在就必須依靠自己去修煉，以及應用所學的一

切，才會有進益。不如你加入我的商隊，跟我回家，我好想

你成為我的兄弟！」

米拉其實願意接納這邀請，他知道康巴族很富裕，因為

他們控制着幾條往中國通商的路綫，但他還是拒絕了，因為

他媽媽的緣故。如果他加入商隊，放棄黑魔法，媽媽可能會

自殺，她曾揚言威脅過。

Then the Lama announced that they had completed their studies and, as a parting gift, he gave each of them a fine woollen coat made of excellent cloth woven in the district. Mila was well aware that what he had learned from the Lama could not provide the dramatic revenge demanded by his mother; he feared to return home empty-handed, and worried that his mother would certainly kill herself as she had vowed. The other disciples made ready to leave, prostrating themselves before the Lama, each offering their master a parting gift before starting homeward.

To see his friends off, Mila put on his new coat and accompanied them out of the village. He said farewell, and then retraced his steps to Yungtun's house, built on high ground overlooking the river. On his way up, Mila collected dried cow dung lying on the road and put the pieces in the lap of his robe. He went into the garden, dug holes under the fruit trees and buried the fertilising manure.

From the roof of his house, Yungtun saw Mila's deeds, and said to Yanchela, "Among all the pupils I have had or ever will have, Mila will always be the most industrious and affectionate. He didn't say farewell to me this morning, apparently because he was returning. When he first came here, he presented me with all he had, even his very self, body and life. The others presented me with some of their money only. What a simple

喇嘛宣佈他們已畢業，更送每人一件這裏著名的特產羊毛袍子，作為臨別的禮物。米拉明知他學會的魔法並不足以為他母親復仇，他更怕空手回家，怕他媽媽會當着他的面自殺，這是她曾發誓過的。門徒都已準備好離去，他們跪別喇嘛又獻上離別的禮物。

米拉穿上新袍子，到村口送別他的同門，然後走回永敦巴的家，那是建在高地，俯瞰河流的一座房子。他一路收集地上的乾牛糞，用袍子下擺盛着，然後他走入花園，在果樹下挖些洞，把牛糞埋在土裏作肥料。

永敦巴在屋頂看着米拉走回來，他對賢切拉說：「我所有的門徒中，米拉是最好的，無論現在或將來都不會找到比他更好的了！從開始，他就奉獻一切給我，不僅是他的財物，甚至他的生命！其他人只奉獻了金錢。他是多麼純真！

nature! He asked to learn black magic to wreak revenge on some relatives who had stolen his family's fortune and made his mother destitute."

"If he is telling the truth," Yanchela said, "it would be a shame, even cruel, not to teach him the arts. We must find out the real circumstances and help him if he deserves it." The twins overheard this conversation and reported it to Mila, who was filled with joy at the prospect of finally receiving the instruction he sought.

When Mila came to him early next morning, Yungtun said, "Well, Thopaga, why have you not gone home yet?"

Mila had folded up his special coat and now he presented it back to his Guru as a fresh gift, bowing deep, with reverence, touching Yungtun's feet. "Oh, Venerable Guru, I have only my mother and a sister. Before his death, my father entrusted my uncle and aunt with our care and also with all of our property. Helped by the neighbours, they have robbed us of everything and ill-treated us beyond endurance. We found no way to redress the injustice done to us. Mother spent all that she had to send me away to learn the black arts. If I return unable to wreak vengeance on our enemies, my mother will certainly commit suicide, so I do not dare go home. I entreat you to teach me the arts for this purpose."

Yungtun asked Mila to tell him the whole story. With tears

他要求學會黑魔法為他母親復仇，用來對付那些奪去他家財產，令他母親赤貧的親戚。」

賢切拉說：「如果他所說的是真實，而你又不肯傳授黑魔法給他，那多麼殘忍，會是遺憾的事！我們一定要找出實情，看他是否值得幫助。」小姊妹無意中聽到他們的談話，就趕忙告訴米拉。米拉非常雀躍，他終於能學到他所渴望的黑魔法了！

第二天一早，當米拉去見永敦巴時，他說：「特巴加為什麼你不回家去？」

米拉把那件新袍子摺好，當作他回贈喇嘛的禮物，恭敬地跪下，以頭觸及永敦巴的腳，說道：「最尊敬的喇嘛，我家只有母親和妹妹。父親在臨終時，委託伯父和姑母照顧我們，又讓他們管理我家所有財產，直至我成年。他們卻搶奪了我們所有財物，更不斷虐待我們，鄰人也是幫凶，我們母子無法伸冤！媽媽耗盡所有，送我出來學黑魔法，如果我回家但無力報仇的話，我媽會自殺的！所以我不敢回家，我懇求您傳授黑魔法給我！」

永敦巴問米拉整件事的經過，米拉淚流滿面帶着哽咽，

streaming and a voice broken by sobs, Mila related all that had happened from the time of his father's death, how they had been defrauded and ill-treated by his Uncle and Aunt.

Yungtun was deeply moved. "If what you have told me is true, then you have been treated most cruelly and unjustly indeed. If I am satisfied that there is sufficient cause, I will allow you to use the black arts for vengeance. I cannot provide the essential teaching to anyone unless I am certain that the arts will be applied justly and not be abused. Many have appealed to me to teach them; countless treasures and gold, silk and tea-bricks from the south, herds of cattle and ponies from the north have poured in as offerings to me in exchange for the peerless arts. None so far have shown true sincerity as well as sufficient cause. However, from the beginning, you have offered your life to me, so I will make full enquiries into your case."

Darma, head of the disciples, was able to do the miraculous Bonn walk and move faster than a horse. He was sent to Mila's hometown to make enquiries about Mila's personal history. After a few days, he came back and confirmed that all Mila had said was true.

Yungtun was then convinced it was an act of justice to bestow the knowledge of the black arts on Mila. "I have withheld the arts from you," he told Mila, "because I feared you did not have sufficient cause for exercising them. Since you

訴說出從他父親臨終到他們被伯父和姑母詐騙和虐待的事。

永敦巴深深的被感動了，說：「如果你所說是真實的，那麼你們受到很大的冤屈！如果我認為有充份的原因，我會允許你施黑魔法來復仇。我不能隨便教人，必須要確知黑魔法不會被誤用作不公正的事。曾經有很多人求我教他們：南方來的人獻給我金、銀、財寶以及絲綢和茶磚，北方來的人獻上成群的牛羊，為的是換取這蓋世無敵的黑魔法。至今無人是真心又有真正的原因。既然從一開始你就奉獻你的生命給我，我會全面調查你的事。」

只有首徒達爾瑪能走波因疾步，他走得比奔馬更迅速。他被指派到米拉的家鄉去查詢米拉的經歷。幾天後他回來了，並確認米拉所說的屬實。

永敦巴然後認為自己應當傳授黑魔法給米拉，「我一向都沒有傳授給你，就是怕你沒有充分的因由去行使黑魔法。

were telling the truth, I shall teach you in full, but you must go to another place for the instruction. I've learned from the Devil himself the most destructive black magic, Purple Basilisk, potent enough to paralyse and kill. I am most reluctant to exercise it, so I have taught it to my good friend, Yonton of Khulung, in exchange for his magic.

"He has taught me how to launch a hailstorm and guide it with a single finger-tip, which I teach exclusively to disciples. He teaches the art of killing to those approved by me. I shall send you to him with my recommendation."

Yungtun sent Darma as a guide and provided Mila with a yak-load of presents, including food and fine woollen cloth, and a letter of recommendation bound up in a white hada. They set off immediately and soon arrived at Khulung.

既然你所說是事實，我會全部教你，但你要去另處學習。我從魔鬼那裏學到最厲害的魔法，『紫龍術』是有強力殺生和令人癱瘓的魔法，我極不願意行使它，因此我和我的好朋友，古龍村的容東交換法術。他教我如何呼喚冰雹，然後用手指去控制它，這法術就由我專門傳授。而他就教殺戮的法術給那些由我指定的門徒，我將推薦你到他那裏。」

永敦巴指派達爾瑪為米拉作嚮導，又提供了禮品，滿載在犛牛背上，包括有：食物、精緻的羊毛編織及一封推薦書，用白色哈達（長絲巾）裹着。他們立即出發，很快就到達古龍村。

Chapter 11
GURU OF THE BLACK ARTS

At Khulung, Mila and Darma asked the villagers where to find Lama Yonton and were directed to his house. The Lama's wife met them at the door and admitted them immediately. When they came into the hall, Mila saw a corpulent but dignified Lama with drooping eyelids sitting on a stack of two cushions covered by a carpet. Mila offered him the yak and its load as a present, and explained that he had been recommended by Lama Yungtun to learn the black arts, in order to take revenge on his Uncle and Aunt.

After listening to the whole story, Yonton said, "I see that you have sufficient cause for learning the black arts, and I will prove my friendship to Lama Yungtung by teaching you. However, only those chosen by the deities can be initiated to Purple Basilisk, the most formidable art. Purple Basilisk would give you the power to command local gods and spirits, even demons from the underworld, and take the lives of people hundreds of miles away."

Mila bowed deeply, touching Yonton's feet. "Venerable Guru, I entreat you to teach me Purple Basilisk. It's the only way to avenge the sufferings of my mother!"

"For the chosen and gifted and, more importantly, those

第十一章
黑魔法大師

到了古龍村，米拉和達爾瑪在村民的指引下找到容東喇嘛的住所。喇嘛的妻子在門口迎接，請他們進入大廳。米拉看到一位莊嚴、頗肥胖的喇嘛，他半垂着眼簾，跌坐在用地毯蓋着的兩個墊子上。米拉送上見面禮，就是犛牛和它背負的物品。說明自己是永敦巴推薦的，來跟他學習黑魔法，為了要向他的伯父和姑母報復。

容東聽過米拉一家的經歷後說：「你顯然是應當學習黑魔法的！看在我的好朋友永敦巴份上，我會教你。但只是被神選中的人，才可以學會『紫龍術』。那是最厲害的黑魔法，能驅使地仙，甚至呼喚地獄裏的魔鬼，更可以在百里外取人性命。」

米拉躬身直至頭觸及容東的腳說：「尊貴的喇嘛，我懇請您傳授『紫龍術』給我，除此我就沒法去為我媽媽伸冤！」

「最先決的條件就是這人必須是命中注定要當巫師，這

destined to be sorcerers, Purple Basilisk is not difficult to acquire. Some hear the doctrine in the morning, meditate on it during the day and learn it by the evening." He gave Mila the necessary instructions and then took him to a cell in the basement of his house to meditate.

Mila was elated. "I must be one of the chosen. Several of my forefathers were famous sorcerers." Feeling comfortable, he sometimes dozed off during meditation. After seven days, Yonton sent for him and asked whether there had been any sign or manifestation. "None whatsoever," Mila replied.

Yonton was disappointed. "There is some obstruction in your karma. You are obviously not among the favoured and gifted. However, we can still supplicate the deities to grant your desired vengeance. We must offer a sacrifice and I shall intercede for you."

While they waited for a full moon under which to hold the rite, all the disciples were kept busy with elaborate preparations. They began by gathering many thorny branches from the black pine to fence in the sacrificial ground, then made a central altar from a pile of black stones and wood, with a human skull placed on top. They used flour to sculpt the form of a large deer and left it to harden in the sun. A collection of animals to be sacrificed included a black dog, a red mare and a yak. The legs of the animals would be broken just before the ceremony. During the

比由神選定，或者是有天份都更重要。『紫龍術』並不難掌握，有人在早上學到經文，只在日間修練，到傍晚就已經掌握了。」他傳授米拉一些重要的經文和修煉的方法，然後帶他到地庫的一間靜室，讓他獨自修習。

米拉有點飄飄然，他想：「我當然是被神選中的，我的幾個祖先都是有名的巫師。」他覺得挺輕鬆，在修習時，偶然也會打瞌睡。容東在七天後請他過去，問他有什麼預兆，或者是跡象。他回答：「完全沒有！」

容東相當失望：「一定是你命中有障礙，顯然你沒有天賦又不受青睞。不過我們仍然可以求神替你伸冤，讓你報復你的仇人。我們必須獻祭，我會盡力為你請求！」

祭祝儀式要等到滿月才舉行，門徒都忙於籌備工作。首先他們採集了很多帶刺的黑松樹枝，編織成籬笆把場地圈出。然後用黑色的石塊和木塊堆一個祭壇在當中。壇頂放置一顆人類的頭骨，用麵粉塑成一隻大鹿讓太陽把它曬得乾硬。預備有三隻犧牲的動物：黑狗、紅母馬和犛牛。等到舉行儀式時，這些動物的腿會被打斷，祭祀時就會屠殺動物，

sacrifice, the animals would be killed and their blood collected in large bronze vessels. The intestines, the most valuable parts, would be used to encircle the piles of food offerings.

On the night of the full moon, the disciples played their instruments. The hills resounded with the music of horns, drums, cymbals and conch shells. Aromatic branches were kept burning for incense. The disciples chanted in unison and danced the mystic three steps around and around the altar. At the climax, the animals were sacrificed. The blood was collected and poured to on the ground as a libation. Yonton mounted the artificial deer and cried, "Ala-la-laa." Mila mounted a large drum and, along with the disciples, wailed and danced frantically until finally they were all spent and fell to the ground.

The next morning, Yonton gave Mila fresh instructions and took him to a cave in the mountain nearby. Mila was sealed up in this cave to meditate. Food was brought to him each day. Chastened by his recent failure, he tried to meditate with the required concentration, but it was difficult for him to stay awake all the time. Once when he was about to doze off, he saw Yonton coming out of the rock wall. The Lama said, "You are supplicating the deities to grant you vengeance. Do you really want this with all of your heart and soul? The deities will not favour a half-hearted request." Yonton turned his back and left through the wall.

把血液儲在大銅盆裏，然後倒在地上奠酒。腸子是最有價值的部份，會用來圍繞一堆堆供奉的食物。

等到月圓的晚上，門徒奏起樂器。群山迴應着喇叭、鼓、鈸和海螺的樂聲，燃燒着的大把松枝發放芳香。他們齊聲唱誦，又繞着圈跳神秘的三步舞。進入高潮時，動物被獻祭，然後用收集的血液倒在地上奠酒。容東騎着鹿像高喊：「啊一拉一拉一啊！」米拉也騎着大鼓和門徒一起尖叫。大家瘋狂的跳舞，直至精疲力盡，倒在地上。

第二天早上，容東給米拉新的指示，帶他到附近的山洞。米拉被關閉在洞穴裏默禱，每天有人送食物給他。米拉曾經失敗，得到教訓，特別聚精會神的打坐，但他卻很難控制自己整天保持清醒。正當他要打瞌睡時，他看見容東穿過岩壁走出來，對他說：「你現在祈求諸神賜給你復仇。你是否真的全心全意？神是不會答允那些沒有誠意的請求的。」容東轉身穿牆離去。

Mila rubbed his eyes, unsure if he were dreaming or not, but meditated with renewed fervour. After forty-nine days, the seal to the cave was broken and Mila came out of the retreat. He had still received no sign from the deities.

"You can make one last appeal," Yonton said. "If you fail, then you must go back to Yuntung and tell him everything. He must understand that I have done all I can to help you and have withheld nothing."

He took Mila to a mountain ridge and pointed out a spot. "You must build a strong cell there that, without tools, no one can pull down easily. It should have three stories underground, and a main floor at ground level built with strong wooden beams, closely fitted. Where the walls meet, the outer corners must be protected with stones as large as the body of a yak. The entrance should be concealed, so that no one can find or force his way in. Above all, you must do everything single-handed, without any help."

Mila immediately commenced with the foundations, labouring from dawn till dusk, digging and filling baskets with earth and stones, then dragging them out with a rope over his shoulder. In a week, he had a running wound on his back where the rope had burned. He switched to the other shoulder and another sore soon developed. After a month, his back was a mess of sores, oozing blood and pus. Undaunted, he continued

米拉揉揉眼睛，不知自己是否發夢，卻使他重新提起精神去默禱。四十九天後，洞穴被打開，米拉出關了，但還是沒有任何跡象。

「你可以作最終的祈求，」容東說：「但如果失敗了，你就要回去找永敦巴，告訴他我們所做的一切。他必須知道我已出盡全力幫你！並沒有任何保留。」

容東帶米拉去山脊，指出一處說：「你要在這裏建一間密室，要有深入地下三層的地牢，地面的主層由結合緊密的樑和柱支撐，外牆的轉角位有羣牛般大的石塊護着，隱蔽的入口，不易被人發現或者闖入。最重要的，就是你必須獨力建造，不得有任何人幫助。」

米拉立即開始造地基，從早到晚不停的挖掘，他把一根繩子拖着一籃又一籃的泥和石，利用肩膀來拉動。一星期後，繩子的磨擦令他的背出現潰瘍。他轉到另一邊的肩膀，但很快又受傷了。一個月後，他的背上長滿了滲膿、血的瘡，但他並不氣餒，只是改變方法，在胸前捧着籃子。

by carrying the basket in front.

Finally, the underground structure was completed and only the ground floor was left to finish. Yonton came several times to check on his progress, and the disciples visited him daily to bring him food and cheer him on.

One day, three disciples came to visit, bringing a large round boulder to be used in sporting activities that they left behind. Seeing it was just what he needed for a corner stone, Mila set it over the foundation by the front door. When Yonton came the next time, Mila was already working on the roof. Yonton pointed at the boulder and frowned. "Where did you get this?"

Mila had to admit that it had been brought uphill by the other disciples and he had used it. Yonton said, "Take it out immediately and restore it to where it came from!" To remove the stone, Mila had to break up two mud walls, a considerable setback. He carefully rolled the stone downhill and then pushed it back to its original spot.

"Now bring the stone back and set it up as before," Yonton said. Mila obeyed his Guru, but tears of despair welled up as, somehow, the stone grew heavier and wouldn't budge, no matter how hard he pushed. Using his utmost strength, he suddenly pried it loose and it rolled away. Lo and behold, a young boy emerged from where the stone had been! About eight years old,

地牢終於建好了，只餘地面的一層。容東來過幾次檢查他的進展，他的同門每天都帶些食物來探望和鼓勵他。

有一天，三位同門來過，留下一塊他們帶來玩遊戲的大圓石。米拉覺得它很適合作基石，就把它安裝在門口。當容東再來時，米拉已經在建造屋頂。容東皺起眉頭，指着大圓石問：「你在哪裏找到的？」

米拉承認是由同門帶上山的，他覺得合適就採用了。容東說：「立刻挖出來，搬回原處！」米拉要打掉兩堵牆才把圓石挖出，是倒退的工作。他小心把石頭滾下山，推回原處。

容東說：「現在把那塊石再搬回去，裝好在之前的位置。」米拉遵循他的意思做，但失望的眼淚快要湧出來了。不知為什麼，石頭越變越重，無論他如何用力的推，石頭都不能稍微的被移動。用盡最大的力氣，石頭突然被撬鬆了，跟着滾開。哎喲！瞧！一個大約八歲的小男孩從石後崩出來，像是

he appeared to be made of threads of rainbow light. For a few moments, he held his hands in front, palms together, in a blessing, and then gradually faded away. Mila knew that his guardian angel had come to console him and felt much encouraged.

由千條彩虹光線造成的。他雙手胸前合十，像祝福的樣子，一會兒就逐漸消失了。米拉知道是他的守護神來安慰他，令他感到鼓舞。

Chapter 12

THE VISITATIONS

After several months of hard labour, Mila completed the building. He was again sealed up for meditation, this time in the underground chamber that he himself had built. This time he could not fail! So that his concentration would not falter, he placed a lighted butter lamp on his head and sat up very straight. Night and day, he meditated, refilling the lamp when it went out, willingly enduring all for his mother's sake. As days passed, he was surprised to experience a lightness that gave him more and more relief. Gradually, his troubles were left behind and he felt tranquil.

His mind roamed free. He saw himself with Peta, romping together in the house and fields, wearing fine clothes and jewelry, with plenty to eat and drink. Those were happy days, he sighed. He then saw his father, in the midst of family and friends, so proud of his house, his fields, herds and all his treasures. It was only a passing show; all that wealth had vanished like morning dew! Now, he saw clearly that the revenge so much desired by his mother would not benefit her at all, either spiritually or materially. Revenge was also an illusion. As the light grew to be a constant stream, he forgot all his worries, his pain, and even his affection for his mother and sister.

第十二章
魔域來客

米拉努力工作了數月，終於把密室建成。他再次閉關在地下室，下了決心只許成功，不許失敗！為了要專注不分心，他把一盞點亮的酥油燈放在頭頂，挺直腰的趺坐着。他日以繼夜在苦修，燈滅了就再添油。他為了母親，甘願受苦。日子一天天過去，他驚訝的感到自己越來越寬心，漸漸地他把煩惱都拋在腦後，變得平靜了。

他的心靈不受拘束，正在漫遊！他看見自己和妹妹百德，在屋裏和田裏嬉戲，穿戴華麗，又有豐富的飲食。他嘆息着緬懷過去的好日子！然後他看見父親，正在親朋中炫耀他的房子、田地和財寶。人生如逝水！他們所有的財富都如朝露般消失了。他清楚知道報仇也是虛幻的，雖然他媽媽渴望着報復，但這不會令她得益，不會有任何精神上或物質上的好處。他覺得正在光浴，漸漸地他忘卻所有的煩惱、痛苦，甚至對他母親和妹妹的愛。

He wanted to dwell in this beautiful state of mind and enjoy the peace that passed understanding. He meditated on and on. Suddenly he was disrupted by a deep, resonant voice calling out his name. "Mila Thopaga, Mila Thopaga!" He passed mysteriously through the walls and stood outdoors in the cold night air. A figure clothed in black sat on a tall dark horse with black hooves. His face was black like coal, and he wore a black feather on his head. He said, "Follow me!" A horse trotted out of the darkness, and Mila climbed on its back. Together they galloped away towards an unknown destination.

Mila felt as if he was airborne, but still, he faintly recognised the passing terrain. When they reached the top of a mountain, the weather suddenly turned much worse, with thunder and lightning and torrential rain. The mountain itself seemed to be trembling. Water streamed down the slopes and the bottom of the valley became a whirling pond that quickly grew into a large lake with churning waves. Just as the road ahead dipped into the valley, an avalanche of hundreds of loose rocks flew through the air. Terror stricken, Mila forcefully reined in his galloping horse and was thrown over its head. He fell down, down, as if dropped from the sky, and believed he was in the land of the dead.

Waking up was slow and painful. Mila found himself back in his cell, and lay there abject with defeat until he heard his

　　他想留住這美妙的境界，又享受着不可思議的寧靜，因此他堅持不斷的修煉。突然他被打斷了！有一把深沉、洪亮的聲音，正在呼喚他：「米拉特巴加、米拉特巴加！」他不知不覺穿越牆壁，發現自己站在戶外的冷空氣裏。一個黑衣人騎着高頭大黑馬，他的臉如煤炭，頭上戴一根黑羽毛。他說：「跟我來！」又另有一匹馬從黑暗中緩緩走出來，讓米拉騎上馬背。他們一起奔馳向未知的目的地。

　　米拉感覺好像在空中飛翔，但他還是依稀認出經過的地形。當他們到達山頂時，天氣突然變得非常惡劣：行雷閃電又下暴雨，連山都像在顫抖。水不停瀉下斜坡，流到谷底，收集成為一個有漩渦的塘，很快就變成波濤翻滾的大湖。當他們沿着斜路進入山谷時，突然雪崩！無數的石塊在空中飛落，米拉被嚇壞了，他極力勒停奔馬，反而被拋過馬頭，翻滾向下。好像從天空自由跌落，他相信已到了死亡之地！

　　帶着疼痛緩緩的醒來，米拉發現自己在地下室裏。他沒精打采，絕望地躺着，直至他聽見同門在外面呼喚，叫他去

friends calling him from outside. His Guru had summoned him. Mila went out from the cell. Yonton said, "Do not be frightened by appearances, for whatever appears is in your own mind. You must neither accept nor reject your vision. To drive away your fear, you must meditate upon the deities and keep repeating the Words of Power. Go back to meditate again."

Mila knew he'd be given a second chance; he was encouraged by his Guru's words. This time he would heed Yonton's advice and not panic.

He placed the lighted lamp on his head and meditated with renewed zeal. Sure enough, the mysterious messenger came to call, and again they galloped away towards the unknown. Again they rode into a storm. This time Mila took it all calmly: thunder, lightning, shrieking wind above, the churning waves below. He rode through the avalanche, although he felt the rocks were tearing at his flesh and breaking his bones. After the turbulence, it became completely calm. He rode for a long time across a vast plateau, keeping pace with his guide in the dark, not knowing if he would ever reach a destination.

He saw something on the horizon. He recognised the silhouette of a castle, glowing with an eerie green light. As he approached, he was shocked to discover that it was completely covered with skulls, both human and animal. The castle stood in a pond of blood that emitted a terrible stench. A drawbridge was

見喇嘛。容東說:「不要害怕見到的現象!其實所有的現象都發自你的內心,你不要信任或拒絕所顯現的一切事物。你想克服恐懼心,就必須相信神又不停的唸大力金剛咒,回去再修煉吧。」

得到容東的鼓勵,米拉知道他會有第二次機會。這次他定會聽從喇嘛的話,不會再恐懼。

他把點着的酥油燈放在頭頂,重新煥發熱情去修煉。不出他所料,那神秘的使者重來,他們又再奔向未知的領域。他們再次遇上風暴,這次他從容面對:雷、電、天空咆哮的風聲、下面翻騰的波浪。他冷靜的騎過雪崩,雖然他感到石塊打來,好像撕裂他的肉,又敲斷他的骨。風暴過後,一切歸於平靜。他們騎過廣闊的高原,在黑暗中他竭力跟上他的嚮導,雖然不知會否到達目的地。

他見到地平線上有些東西,然後他認出這是一個城堡的輪廓,泛着詭異的綠光。當他走近時,他震驚地發現這城堡的外牆滿鋪着人頭骨!一池血水圍繞着城堡,發出陣陣腥

lowered for them and the Guide rode into the Castle, beckoning Mila to follow. Mila dared not, for this must be the Kingdom of Mara. If he went in, his soul would be possessed and he would be enslaved for all eternity.

He rolled off the saddle and knelt in the dust, repeating the Words of Power and knocking his head on the ground until blood streamed down his face. When day broke, he fainted several times in the sun's heat but was refreshed by occasional showers. Day passed into night and night into day, yet still he knelt by the pond of blood, keeping up the kow-tow as much as he was able. There was no retreat, and he expected to die there, for he would not give up his own soul.

Suddenly, there was an ear-splitting peal of thunder. Mila looked up, welcoming rain, but the sky was empty, the brilliance blinding. In one huge flash, the light consumed everything. All turned into dust, and the world was no more!

臭！吊橋放下讓他們進城，使者先騎進入，用手勢召喚<u>米拉</u>跟隨他的馬。<u>米拉</u>卻不敢，這裏定是魔王的國度，如果他走進去，他的靈魂就會被魔鬼佔領，永遠做奴隸！

他從馬鞍滾下，跪在塵土中，唸着<u>大力金剛咒</u>，不停的叩頭在地，直到血流到他的臉。在白天，他數次昏倒在熾熱的陽光中，又被驟雨淋醒。從白天到晚上，一天又一天，他還是跪在血池邊，竭力地叩頭。已經沒有退路了，他預計會死在那裏，但他絕不會放棄自己的靈魂！

突然一陣震耳的雷聲，<u>米拉</u>往上望，他想天色要下雨了！但天上一片虛空，明亮得令人目眩！然後是極燦爛的閃電，一切都消失在輻射光中，所有都變成塵土，這世界已不存在了。

Chapter 13
REVENGE

When he woke, Mila found himself lying on the floor of his cell, with his Guru watching over him. He scrambled quickly to a kneeling position. To his astonishment, Yonton said, "Your prayer has been granted! Know that your wish is fulfilled. Tonight, keep watch at the altar and you will see the fruits of your success."

Doubting very much that it could be true, Mila prepared an offering and knelt all night at the ground-floor altar he had built. Towards dawn, he heard a long peal of thunder and then lighting struck the end of the altar. In a flash, Mila saw about thirty bleeding heads lying in a heap, like trophies. In another smaller heap were the bleeding hearts. He recognised the faces of most of his enemies; however, his Uncle and Aunt were missing. A small voice said succinctly in his ear, "Is this what you want? You've called upon us so piteously, over and over."

The next morning, he told Yonton of his vision. Yonton said, "Your Uncle and Aunt ought to be sacrificed. Do you want them killed?"

Mila thought for a moment. His uncle and aunt were his worst enemies, but he realised that he no longer thirsted for their blood. He prayed that they would be spared and bear witness to

第十三章
復仇

米拉醒來發現自己躺在密室的地上，容東正看着他，他趕忙爬起又跪着。出乎他的意料，容東竟說：「天神已經答允你的祈求，你已得償所願！今夜你守着祭壇，就會見到成果。」

米拉雖然滿腹疑惑，還是準備好祭品，整夜跪在他所建的祭壇邊。天快亮時，一陣震耳的隆隆雷聲，閃電好像擊中壇底。閃光中他看到大約三十個淌血的頭顱，像戰利品般堆起，旁邊有一小堆血淋淋的心。他認出都是他敵人的臉，但其中卻沒有他的伯父和姑母！有人悄悄在他耳邊清楚的說：「你可憐巴巴地一遍又一遍呼喚我們，這就是你想要的嗎？」

第二天早上他告訴容東他所見到的願景。容東說：「你的伯父和姑母應要被犧牲的，你要殺他們嗎？」

他的伯父和姑母都是他最恨的仇人，但他意識到自己不想殺死他們，他只求神饒他們的命，好讓他們見證恢恢的天網！

the justice of the deities.

"Stay here with me," Yonton said. "You won't have to wait long before you learn what has taken place."

One evening, a while later, when Mila came back from the fields, he found his old nurse, Urmo, waiting for him. She had walked for a month, searching the countryside, making enquiries. Urmo had been sent by his mother to warn him of the impending danger to his life, and she told Mila that many villagers had been killed in a recent disaster.

She described how, on the night of a wedding feast at his Uncle's house to celebrate his son's marriage, many close friends and relatives came early to the party. They were already enjoying the food and drinks before the other guests arrived. Nurse went out to fetch some water from the well, but when she looked back towards the house, she was greatly shocked. The ground floor stable, usually full of horses, was covered with crawling snakes, spiders and scorpions, even croaking frogs! A monstrous scorpion tugged at the central pillar, as if to pull it down. She screamed, dropped her pail and started to run. She hardly had time to escape before she was stopped short by hearing a loud bang, and turned to see the whole house come crashing down.

Later, Urmo said, she discovered the real cause of the disaster. A large number of horses tied up in the stable became

容東說：「你停留在我這裏吧！不久你就會知道發生了什麼事。」

一個黃昏當米拉從田裏回家，發現老奶娘等待着他。她在鄉下到處尋找詢問，步行差不多一個月才找到他。米拉的媽媽要奶娘來警告他：提防有性命危險！她又告訴他最近家鄉發生了災難，有許多人喪生。

她描述了如何：當夜是伯父兒子的婚宴，雖然宴會還未開始，那些至親好友提早到來享用酒菜。奶娘走到井邊打水，當她回頭望向房子時，她被嚇壞了！本來馬廐裏有很多馬匹，現在卻爬滿了蠕動的蛇、蜘蛛、蠍子，甚至蛤蟆！一只蠍子怪物正在拉扯着當中的大柱，像要拉倒它。她尖叫着把水桶掉下，正要逃跑，轟然一聲巨響令她停步，回頭看見整座房倒塌下來！

奶娘說：後來她才找到這場災難的真正原因。馬廐裏很多拴着的馬變得激動起來，有幾只小馬掙脫了繩索衝向母

agitated and several colts got loose. They rushed at the mares, stirring up a great turmoil of neighing and kicking. One mare gave such a terrific kick at the main pillar that it broke and the whole house tumbled down. The tremendous crash raised a thick cloud of smoke and dust. The ruin was filled with the bodies of men, women, children and animals. Among the thirty-five dead were the bride and Uncle's four sons, as well as Uncle and Aunt's close friends and allies.

Fortunately, the other guests had lingered on their way from the village, walking leisurely and talking, and were spared. They had been saying, "How true goes the proverb: 'Trust someone with your house and you will be turned out of your home!' Even if Thopaga can't achieve vengeance by means of black magic, it's high time for these people to get their comeuppance. Believe in karma and we'll see them punished soon for their wickedness." They arrived just in time to witness the catastrophe. Some were shocked and stunned, while others cried out and started wailing.

Peta heard the noise and came out of the house to check, then rushed back to tell her mother. "Uncle's house has fallen down and a lot of people have been killed!"

Doubting that it was true, White Garland got up and went to have a look. When she saw the ruin covered with fire and smoke, and people wailing and crying, she became mad with

馬，引起騷動，馬兒嘶叫着亂踢。一隻母馬強力的踢向主柱，把它踢斷了，整座房子就倒塌下來。現場佈滿濃濃的煙塵，到處都是屍體！其中有男、女、小孩和動物。最後計數，共有三十多人死去，包括：新娘、伯父的四個兒子和他的至親好友。

其他賓客幸而免於災難，他們一起從村子慢慢走過來，一路在閒談。有人說：「諺語說得對，『讓他人托管你的房子，到頭來你就被趕出你的家』就算特巴加不能用黑魔法報復，也該是報應的時辰了，天網恢恢！我們就快會見到這些邪惡的人得到懲罰！」他們及時來到，見證了災難！有些被嚇呆了，亦有人哀號、哭泣！

百德聽到嘈雜聲，跑出去看，回來告訴她媽媽：「伯父的房子倒塌了，死了很多人！」

白花冠很是懷疑，她起身出去看過究竟。當她見到冒着煙火的廢墟和那些號哭的人群，殘酷的喜悅令她變得瘋狂

cruel joy. She rushed home, tied a rag on top of a long pole and raised it like a banner. She ran back to the scene and paraded to and fro, muttering to herself and stopping to stare at the ruin every now and then.

"Glory to the gods and all hail to the gurus!" she cried. "Did not Mila Sherab have a worthy son? Have I not avenged myself? I've had to wear rags and eat coarse food for years, but it was worth it to see this. 'Fight if strong and curse if weak!' This was Uncle's challenge to us. Has this challenge been answered? The curse of the weak and few have now overcome the mighty and many!' She raved on and on. "Look at the bodies of men and women above and animals below. Look at the provisions and treasures all spoiled. Oh, my son has done this for me and blessed my old age! How delighted I am to enjoy this moment of perfect triumph!" Peta was unable to stop her; eventually her brother, Thangme, arrived, took her hand and forcefully led her home.

Everyone heard White Garland's gloating, and even her friends thought she had gone too far. Vengeance was enough; she should not give way to such excessive ill-will. When news of White Garland's behaviour reached the ears of the relatives and friends of the victims, they were enraged. They said, "Not only was she responsible for the terrible death and destruction of so many, but she also boasted of her triumph. Let's wring out her

了！她趕回家，把抹布縛在一根長竹竿頂，高高舉起它像一面旗幟。她趕回現場，在那裏走來走去，一面喃喃自語，不時站定盯着廢墟。

「榮耀歸於神，向喇嘛敬禮！」她喊叫着：「看<u>誰熱嘉參</u>有個好兒子！看我不是報了仇！雖然多年來我穿破衣服吃粗糧，但只看到今天這樣就是值得的！『你有力量就來爭鬥，是弱小就只能詛咒！』伯父是這樣挑戰我們！我們是不是回答了這挑戰？今天弱者的詛咒克服了眾多的強者！」她不停的咒罵：「看這堆屍體，在上是男人、女人，在下是畜牲。看這些全壞了的日用品和貴重物品！這都是我兒子為我做的好事啊！讓我老年得福。我大獲全勝，多麼開心！」<u>百德</u>沒法阻止她，結果她的哥哥，<u>唐美</u>來到，握着她的手，強行拉她回家。

所有人聽到<u>白花冠</u>幸災樂禍的話，都覺得她太過份！報復已經足夠了，她不應說這些極端仇恨的話。<u>白花冠</u>的行為很快就傳到死者親友的耳，他們被觸怒了：「她不單只造成許多人死亡、受害，她還要誇耀她的勝利。讓我們絞出她

wicked heart!"

However, the village elders disagreed. "It's not prudent to kill her, for her son may answer by causing another calamity, and perhaps kill us all. We must find the cub first, kill him on the spot, and then deal with the mother."

All agreed to this strategy except Uncle. He said, "I have no more sons or daughters to lose. I welcome death!" He rushed forth to kill White Garland but was held back by the neighbours.

"It was all because of you that we have come to this," the neighbours said. "Now you want to create more mischief? If you act on your own, then we are no longer friends and we'll try to stop you." Uncle had no choice but to submit to the majority.

Thangme spoke severely to White Garland. "Wasn't revenge enough for you? You have already caused them death and destruction. Why announce your hate in such a fashion? Your recklessness is endangering yourself and your son. The neighbours are plotting against you now."

"Oh, brother, you are right!" White Garland wept. "But put yourself in my place. We were cheated of our fortune and treated so badly for all these years. Could anyone help feeling as I did?"

"I understand how you feel," Thangme said, "but I fear for you. Be careful, and lock your doors for murderers may come." As soon as he left, she secured her doors and sat down to think.

Peta was in tears. "Mother, I am so unhappy! Nobody in the

缺德的心！」

但村中的父老不同意：「殺死她是不智的做法！她的兒子可能回報以更大的災禍，或者殺死所有人！我們一定要先找到兒子，當場殺了他，然後再處置他的媽媽！」

所有人都同意，除了伯父說：「我已經沒有兒女了，我想死！」他要衝出去殺白花冠，但被人阻攔了。

村人說：「都是因為你，我們才會這樣淒慘，現在你還要搗亂！如果你一意孤行，你就不再是朋友，我們會制止你的！」伯父無法只得服從大眾。

唐美嚴厲的對白花冠說：「報仇還不夠嗎？你已經造成了死亡和破壞，你為什麼要說那麼仇恨的話？你恣意的行為危及你和兒女！鄰人正在密謀對付你們。」

白花冠哭了：「哥哥你是對的啊！設身處地如果你是我，我們的財產被騙又被虐待多年，誰又能怪我這些感受？」

唐美說：「我理解你的感受，但是我擔心你們。你要小心提防，把門鎖好，可能有人想來殺害你！」他走後她馬上鎖好門，然後坐着思量。

百德流淚說：「媽媽我很不開心！村裏人人都不理睬我。」

village speaks to me anymore."

"Now that's not so," White Garland said. "Zesay is your friend."

"But Zesay lives so far away. Whenever I walk by, people close their doors and windows. The neighbours used to give me odd jobs so that I could earn some money. Now they won't even speak to me. Even Zesay is afraid of walking in the village with me!"

White Garland realised that they were being ostracised and life was becoming more difficult as well as dangerous. "Never mind, these people have no heart. They were so friendly and respectful when we were rich but laughed at us when we became poor. Now they despise and shirk us when we are in trouble."

"We cannot go on like this! What's to be done?"

White Garland grew angry. "They cannot keep trampling on us. Now that Thopaga can work magic, he will show them!"

Meanwhile, Nurse Urmo had learned of the plot to kill Thopaga and was very concerned. She warned White Garland, and agreed to find Thopaga and alert him of the danger. White Garland gave Nurse all she had for the journey, wrote a letter to Thopaga, and gratefully saw her off.

白花冠說：「不會吧！你還有澤思是你的好朋友。」

百德說：「但澤思住得很遠！當我走過，他們都關上門和窗。以前鄰人會給我一些散工，讓我賺點錢。現在他們全不理睬我，就算澤思也怕和我走在一起！」

白花冠明白她們已被村人放逐，以後的日子會更困難，而且會有危險。她說：「不要緊！這些人都沒有心肝，當我們有錢時，他們對我們友好尊重，我們窮了，卻譏笑我們。現在我們有難，他們就鄙視避開我們！」

百德說：「我們不能這樣下去！怎麼辦！」

白花冠生氣了：「他們不可以永遠欺負我們！特巴加現在能行使黑魔法，可以給他們點顏色瞧！」

這時奶娘也得知村人要殺死特巴加的陰謀，她很擔心就告訴白花冠，她願意去找特巴加，警告他有生命危險。白花冠很感激她，傾囊給她旅費，自己寫了一封信給兒子，讓奶娘送去。

White Garland and Her Daughter
母與女

Chapter 14

AFTERMATH

White Garland and Peta lived in fear and loneliness, cut off from the village community. When White Garland thought over her situation, she became increasingly apprehensive of her neighbours. It was little consolation that her life was not in immediate jeopardy, as her enemies' plan was to find and kill Thopaga first and then her. She spent days and some sleepless nights trying to find a way out of her predicament.

Finally, she decided to mount a counter-attack on her enemies, knowing that she and her daughter could not live in constant fear. She would ask Thopaga to strike a blow that would intimidate the villagers forever! She sold the remaining portion of her field, "Little Famine Carpet", for seven gold coins. She wanted to take the gold to Thopaga herself, but was reluctant to leave Peta behind. Then her luck changed, for a messenger came to her door.

Wangdula was a herdsman from the northern highland, on his way back from a pilgrimage to the holy places in Nepal. He came looking for Mila Sherab, with whom he had traded years ago. White Garland remembered that her late husband had mentioned Wangdula favourably. She invited him to stay with her for a few days and did her best to make him comfortable.

第十四章
報仇餘孽

白花冠和百德孤獨地生活在恐懼中，事實上她們已被村人放逐。當白花冠考慮到她現時的情況，她就越來越害怕，幸而她即時沒有性命危險！因為敵人的戰略是要先找到特巴加，殺了他才對付她。她天天擔憂甚至有不眠之夜，不斷的動腦筋想脫離困境。

她想到自己和女兒不能長期過着擔驚害怕的日子，她決定對敵人反攻！她會叫特巴加給村人一個大打擊，讓他們永遠恐懼！她把剩餘的田地「餓荒小地毯」賣掉，得到七枚金幣，她想親自帶去給特巴加，卻不願把百德留在家裏。正在為難，幸而她行好運了！一個信差來到她的家門。

旺都拉是北方高原的牧人，他曾往尼泊爾朝聖，在歸途中，順道來探訪多年前與他交易的誰熱嘉參。白花冠記得她的丈夫曾讚賞過他，她就邀請他留宿幾天，她盛情款待令他感到舒適。從談話中，她覺得旺都拉是老實、可靠的人。她

Through their conversation, she discovered that he was indeed honest and reliable. She wanted him to be her messenger to Thopaga, but she had to make sure. She trimmed a butter lamp and addressed a fervent prayer to the guardian deities of her family, asking for a sign. If the lamp continued to burn for a long time, then it meant Wangdula would deliver her letter safely. If he was not trustworthy, then it would quickly go out. The lamp continued burning for a day and night, so she knew that she had found the right messenger.

She gave him a good piece of cowhide to repair his boots, and also offered to mend his dilapidated blanket cloak. She covered the rents and tears in the cloak with a large piece of material, then sewed on a black square as an ornament. With thick white thread, she embroidered a large six-pointed star on the square, and at each of the six points of the star she put a gold coin and stitched all around it in a star pattern to secure it. The last coin was stitched in at the very centre. The cloak was now ornamented with a pattern of seven stars, a constellation known as the Pleiades. She gave Wangdula a handsome present, requesting him to deliver the sealed letter to Thopaga, and he promised faithfully to do so.

After his departure, White Garland spread a rumour through Peta and Zesay that a letter from Thopaga had been brought by the pilgrim. She forged this letter:

想請他送信給<u>特巴加</u>，但她要確保不會出錯。於是她從新點燃一盞酥油燈，虔誠的向她家的守護神禱告，要求顯示：如果油燈能夠保持燃燒一段長時間，那表示<u>旺都拉</u>會好好把信帶到，但如果他是不可靠的，燈就會很快熄滅。那燈持續燃燒了一晝夜，因此她知道找對了信差！

她送給他一塊上好的牛皮去補他的靴子，又主動提出要為他補好他已殘破的披風。她先用一大幅布蓋着那些裂縫和小洞，然後加上一小方塊黑布作裝飾。她用粗白線繡一大顆六角星在黑布上，又把六枚金幣隱藏在六角尖端，再用星星的圖案縫緊，把最後的一枚金幣縫在正中。披風現在有七星座圖案的裝飾。她送他一份很好的禮物，請他把一密封的信送去給<u>特巴加</u>，他忠實地承諾會送到。

他離去後<u>白花冠</u>就讓<u>百德</u>和<u>澤思</u>散佈謠言說：朝聖者帶來了<u>特巴加</u>的信，她又偽造了這封信：

My dear Mother and Sister,

I hope you are well! You've now seen some proof of my prowess in magic. Is there anyone hostile to you, trying to ill-treat or intimidate you? Just let me know that person's name, his family and his offense to you. I'll simply annihilate them! It's easily done, as easy for me as saying grace before a meal. I would not kill just one or two, but I'd root out the entire family. If the whole community is hostile to you, you should come here to stay with me. I'll then destroy the entire countryside, leaving not a trace of life. You need not have any worries about me. I am living here in ease and comfort, spending my days in the study of the art.

Your devoted son, Thopaga.

Peta showed the letter to several somewhat friendly neighbours, and Zesay let her friends read it. Then it was handed over to Uncle Thangme. Eventually, everyone knew about the letter, and were frightened. After much talk, the elders decided to abandon their plan of murder and instead seek reconciliation with White Garland and her son. They compelled Uncle and Aunt to return the field, "Worma Triangle", to White Garland, which was an important part of their inheritance. White Garland felt relieved that her family was out of danger for the time being.

Following directions from Nurse Urmo, it was not difficult for Wangdula to find Mila at Khulung. He gave Mila the latest news about his mother and sister and handed him the letter. Mila read it eagerly, but found it most perplexing:

親愛的媽媽和妹妹：

你們好！你們已經見證了我施魔法的威力！誰敢與你們為敵、威脅或凌辱你們？你只要告訴我：他的名字，家族和怎麼得罪你們，我就會消滅這人。對我來說這只是輕易的事，就像我飯前唸經般易。我不會只殺一兩個，我是會斬草除根殺全家！如果人人都敵對你們，就應該搬來跟我同住。我就會把鄉下完全摧毀，沒有生還的！你們不用擔心我，我過得自由自在，每天都努力學習魔法。

你的愛兒
特巴加

百德拿這封信給幾個較友善的鄰人看，澤思也讓朋友讀信，接着交信給唐美叔叔，後來所有村人都知道這封信，大家都很害怕。父老們開了幾個會議，最後決定放棄謀殺特巴加的計劃，並且與白花冠和解。他們逼使伯父和姑母把「窩馬三角田」交還白花冠，那是他們應承繼的。白花冠感到自己和兒女目前已脫離危險了。

旺都拉按照奶娘的指示，很快就找到米拉，把信交給他又告訴他，他家裏的最新消息。米拉心急的讀信，但內容卻令他費解：

My Dear Thopaga,

I hope you are in good health. I am so proud of you. You've proved yourself worthy of your noble father, Mila Sherab. Your prowess in black magic was demonstrated here most impressively! Your Uncle's house suddenly collapsed during the wedding party for his son, and thirty-five people were killed. However, people here blame us for the catastrophe. They hate us now and want revenge. They are conspiring to send someone to find and kill you, and then kill myself and your sister. We live in dread and misery. For our sake, you must again exercise your black magic and intimidate them. This is the only way to give us protection. I ask you to launch a terrible hailstorm upon them. I've heard that there are nine different types of hailstorms. Launch one and that would give your old mother complete satisfaction.

Please take very good care of yourself. You are probably running short of money. Look for a valley nearby that is facing north, usually shadowed by a black cloud, and lit at night by a constellation known as the Pleiades. There you will find seven of our relatives and they will provide you with all that you need. If you cannot find the valley, ask the pilgrim who brought you this letter, for he lives in it. Do not enquire of anyone else.

Your loving mother.

Mila knew that his mother was fond of riddles, but this one was really beyond him. He yearned to return home and ensure the safety of his mother and sister, but he was out of money, with no inkling as to where to find these relatives. Close to tears, he kept

親愛的特巴加：

你好嗎？我以你為榮！

你也證明了你配得上你高貴的父親，<u>誰熱嘉參</u>。你的黑魔法本領令這裏的人印象深刻！你伯父的房子突然倒塌，正在他為兒子舉行婚宴時。共有三十五人死亡！然而村人指責我們引起這場災難，他們現在恨我們，想要報復。他們正密謀要派人去殺害你，然後再對付我和你的妹妹。我們生活在恐懼與痛苦中，為了我們着想，你必須再施行黑魔法去恐嚇他們，這是保護我們的唯一方法！我要求你對他們降下可怕的暴雨冰雹！我聽說有九種不同的冰雹，只要降下其中之一，你老母親就滿意了！

請你好好照顧自己！你可能不夠錢用，你去找附近的一個山谷，那是朝北又經常被烏雲遮蓋，但到晚上天空就亮起星星，所謂<u>七宿星座</u>。在那裏你會找到七個我們的親戚，他們會供給你所需的一切。如果你找不到這個山谷，不必詢問其他人，只問帶信給你的朝聖客，因為他住在那裏！

愛你的媽媽

<u>米拉</u>知道媽媽喜歡打謎語，但這信真是令他費解！他渴望回家以確保媽媽和妹妹的安全，但他缺錢，要找到這些親戚又沒有端倪，他幾乎要哭出來了！他不斷詢問<u>旺都拉</u>關於這七

questioning Wangdula about the seven relatives – who they were, where they lived and where Wangdula himself had come from. Wangdula said that he had been to several places but knew nothing of the relatives. He himself was a native of the Province of U. Mila asked him to wait while he showed the letter to his guru.

Mila told his guru the news from home, and Yonton read the letter. "Thopaga, your mother seems very vindictive. So many killed already, yet she still commands you to launch a hailstorm. What relatives do you have in the North?"

"I've never heard of any," Mila said. "I've questioned the pilgrim, but he also knew nothing about them. It's just like my mother to talk in riddles!"

Yonton sent for his wife, saying, "The wit of a woman can best be fathomed by another woman."

She came at once, read through the letter and asked Mila to call in the pilgrim. She then had a big fire made and served him beer. Wangdula soon took off his heavy cloak. She put it on her back playfully, strutting up and down the room. "Happy indeed are the travellers who wander everywhere with no other clothing than this on their back!" She danced a little, then left the room wearing the cloak. Upstairs, she quickly opened the seams, removed the gold coins, and then resewed the cloak and went back downstairs to give it back to the pilgrim.

個親戚：他們是誰？住在那裏？旺都拉自己又是從那裏來的？旺都拉說：他曾去過很多地方，對米拉的親戚卻一無所知！而他的家鄉就是 U 省。米拉請旺都拉逗留片刻，待他拿信去請教喇嘛。

米拉把家鄉的消息告訴容東，他讀信後說：「特巴加，你媽媽是個報復心重的人！這麼多人死亡，她還命令你降一次冰雹！到底你有什麼親戚在這附近？」米拉說：「我從未聽說過！我曾問過朝聖客，但他也是一無所知。我媽就是喜歡打謎語！」

容東派人去請他的妻子來，說道：「只有女子才能揣摩到另一個女子的想法！」

她很快來到，讀了信就叫米拉請朝聖客進來。她生大火使客廳溫暖又請他喝啤酒，旺都拉很快就脫下沈重的披風。她把它披在身上玩，趾高氣揚的上下走着：「快樂的旅人，只穿上這件衣服到處漫遊！」她跳了一會舞，穿着披風走出去。到了樓上，她就迅速打開接縫，取出金幣，再重新縫好，然後她回去把披風還給朝聖客。

When Wangdula was safely lodged, she called to Mila. "Thopaga, your teacher wants to see you." She then handed Mila the seven gold coins.

Mila asked where she had found them, and she replied, "You must have a very shrewd mother. The valley facing north is the pilgrim's cloak, which no sunlight can penetrate. The black cloud refers to the black patchwork and the constellation is represented in the embroidery. The seven relatives are the gold coins. The remark about not enquiring from anyone else save the pilgrim was intended to direct your attention to him and search there."

The guru was very pleased. "Once more, we men can only marvel at the proverbial wit of women."

Mila gave one tenth of a coin to Wangdula, who was delighted, and he also gave part of a coin to the lady and three gold coins to his guru. He entreated Yonton to teach him the art of launching a hailstorm. "I am commanded by my mother."

But Yonton referred him back to Yungtun. "Only he has the right to teach this branch of the black arts." Furnished with a recommendation letter, a white hada and the necessary gift, Mila went back to Yungtun at Yarlung.

當她把旺都拉安頓好後，她叫米拉過來：「特巴加，你的老師想見你。」然後交給他七枚金幣。

米拉問她是如何發現的，她說：「你的媽媽非常精明！向北的山谷沒有陽光滲透，那是朝聖客的披風。黑雲指的是那裝飾的黑方塊，星座就是刺繡圖案，而七個親戚就是七枚金幣。至於不要詢問其他人，只問帶信者，就是要你把注意力放在朝聖客身上！」喇嘛開心的說：「我們男子只得再一次讚嘆女子的聰明智慧！」

米拉把一個金幣分了一點給旺都拉，他高興極了，又把剩餘的送給女士，再獻上三枚給喇嘛。他懇求容東教他降冰雹的法術，說道：「這是我母親的命令。」容東只得轉介他回去找永敦巴，說道：「他是唯一有權教授這門黑魔法的人。」米拉帶着白巾裹着的推薦信和慣例的禮品，再次回到雅龍村、永敦巴的居處。

Chapter 15

HAILSTORM

Yungtung was rather surprised to see Mila returning. Mila presented him with the letter and the white hada from his friend, Yonton, and also offered him the remaining three gold coins. When Yungtung asked about his study with Yonton, Mila told of his success and the story of his vengeance, where thirty-five of his enemies were killed as the result, and now the angry villagers were plotting to murder him and his mother. He showed Yungtung the letter from his mother and begged the guru to teach him the art of launching a hailstorm.

Yungtung said, "You should realise by now that the path of vengeance is perilous! Are you not afraid of the grave consequences?"

"I must obey my mother's command," replied Mila. "Please grant my request." Yungtung reluctantly agreed. For the next month, Mila stayed in an old disused cottage where Yungtun taught him the secret of creating a hailstorm. After this, Mila searched the countryside and found a large rock cave in the face of a cliff. He cleaned it up to make it habitable and then shut himself inside, leaving only a small aperture for receiving food and water.

Mila offered daily prayers and rituals to the deities, and

第十五章
暴雨冰雹

永敦巴見到米拉回來覺得詫異。米拉呈上容東寫的推薦書、帶來的禮物和餘下的三枚金幣。永敦巴問及他跟隨容東的學業。米拉就告訴他：已成功報仇了，在他家鄉有三十多人被誅殺，而現在憤怒的村人正密謀要殺害他和他的媽媽。他讓永敦巴讀媽媽的來信並懇求他傳授驅使雹暴的法術。

永敦巴說：「你現在應該明白復仇是一條兇險的路！難道你不怕會有嚴重後果？」

米拉說：「我一定要遵從媽媽的命令，請你應允我的請求！」永敦巴勉強地答應了。接着的幾個月，米拉住在一所荒廢的農舍，永敦巴就在那裏傳授他冰雹的法術。米拉然後在郊野找到岩壁上的大山洞，打掃乾淨後，他就在封密的洞裏閉關，只通過小窗口來輸送食物。

米拉每天祈禱，供奉神明，其餘時間就冥想，他沒有

meditated. His thoughts did not wander, and his mind stayed in the void. One day he thought he saw some mist gathering at the back of his cave. The mist gradually thickened to form clouds, which grew more dense and black, settling in and filling the whole cave. Suddenly he was in the midst of a hurricane. Ear-splitting noises and hundreds of hailstones battered his body, tearing his skin and breaking his bones. Mila thrashed about frantically and, quite by accident, his hand pointed at the cave's entrance. Following his direction, the storm rushed out, bursting the rocks that sealed the cave. Sucked out by the air current, Mila clung to a big rock and saved himself from falling down the cliff.

He was covered in wounds, yet he did not mind – he was elated, for he had succeeded in calling up a hailstorm! Yungtung said that now he only had to learn how to direct it. For the next month, Mila stood outside his cave and practised calling up a hailstorm, then directing it to dispel itself in the distant wilderness. He told his guru that he was ready to go back home to carry out his mother's request.

"Quite right," Yungtung said. "Now you are able to launch a hailstorm, but tell me – how tall is the barley in your village at this time of the year?"

"Seed is usually sown now," Mila said.

"It's much too early," Yungtung said. "You have to wait."

雜念，心靈一片虛空。有一天他好像看到一團霧在洞的後面，那些霧越來越濃，凝聚成黑雲，漸漸地沉澱，黑色的煙霧充滿了洞穴。突然刮起大風！刺耳的風哨聲，數以百計的冰雹敲打他的身體，好像要他破皮斷骨。他瘋狂地翻來覆去，無意中他的手指指着洞口。風暴跟隨着他指的方向突破密封的洞口衝出去。米拉也被氣流抽走，他緊抱着塊大石才沒有跌下懸崖。

雖然他身上處處都是傷痕，他並不介意，只是感到高興，因為他已成功喚來冰雹。永敦巴說，目前他要學的是如何去指使它。接着的一個月，米拉站在洞外練習喚起冰雹，又指使它在散落在遙遠的荒野。他告訴喇嘛已準備就緒，可以回鄉去履行母親的要求。

永敦巴說：「不錯，你已經能夠驅使雹暴了。但告訴我，你家鄉種的大麥，這時有多高？」

米拉說：「通常這是播種的時候。」

永敦巴說：「還是為時過早！你還得等待。」

As time went by, Mila described to his guru when the young shoots appeared, when the planting was high enough to hide pigeons, and the arrival of the season for weeding. Yungtung listened with interest, but said that it was still too early. Mila kept him informed when the ears appeared. Finally, when the ears were full, Yungtung decided that it was time for Mila to go home to launch the hailstorm. To accompany Mila, he sent Darma who was a powerful fighter and fleet of foot. Disguised as pilgrims, the two arrived at the village, where they found that the golden harvest was more abundant than it had ever been before.

Mila and Darma found lodging in the cottage of an old woman who lived alone on the mountain above the village. She was reclusive, hard of hearing and half-blind, and farmed a small plot at the edge of the village, tending a dozen goats. She told them that the villagers were rejoicing, as this year's harvest had surpassed any in living memory. The village elders had declared that no one should start reaping until a chosen day when all would reap at the same time. Until then they were busy preparing a feast of thanksgiving and celebration.

Early the next morning, Mila went up the mountain and found a secluded spot where he set up his apparatus directly above the village. He chanted and danced, following the ritual taught by his guru. He waited, but the sun shone brightly in the

　　日子一天一天的過去，<u>米拉</u>不時向喇嘛報告：嫩枝長出時，植物長高至能隱藏鴿子時，還有除草的季節到了。<u>永敦巴</u>感興趣去聆聽，但總是說為時過早。<u>米拉</u>照樣告訴他：田裏長滿麥穗時，等到麥穗飽滿時，<u>永敦巴</u>然後認定：這是時候讓<u>米拉</u>回家降雹暴了。他派<u>達爾馬</u>陪伴<u>米拉</u>回去，<u>達爾馬</u>是個強壯鬥士又跑得很快，兩人偽裝為朝聖的香客。到達家鄉時發現田裏大片金黃，今年是罕有的豐收。

　　他們在村外山上小屋留宿，這是位獨居老婦人的家。她已半盲又重聽，生活只靠耕種。她擁有一片小田在村邊，又養十幾頭山羊。她說：村人都很開心，因為今年田裏的豐收是空前的。父老們命令不得獨自收割，要等到選定的吉日才一起收割。目前大家正忙於準備一場盛宴，以慶祝及酬神。

　　第二天<u>米拉</u>早起去爬山，他找到一隱蔽處俯瞰着村子。然後他舉行儀式：舞動着身體，一面誦經又唸咒語。他等待着，但見晴明的天空中，陽光燦爛，連麻雀般大小的雲朵也

clear sky, and not even a sparrow-sized cloud appeared. Feeling desperate, he once more called out the names of the deities, then wept bitterly, beating the earth with his folded robe. He cited aloud the wrongs done to his family and the cruelty of the neighbours.

Soon after, scattered clouds began to appear and gather into one huge black cloud that settled in the sky overhead. Suddenly, lightning flashed and thunder growled and a hailstorm burst forth. All hell broke loose! Hailstones and rain poured down, a strong gale blew, and Mila and his friend ran back to the old woman's cottage for shelter.

They found her weeping loudly and beating her chest. "Oh, my harvest will be ruined! What have I to live on this winter? I shall starve to death."

It was too much for Mila to bear. He couldn't stand to be so cruel to the old woman. He said, "Take this stone and draw your field on the floor." She drew a narrow, elongated shape that Mila quickly covered with his hat, but a small portion was left exposed, as it was too long. Although it was dangerous for him to do so, in his mind he sheltered it from the storm.

When the storm was all over, they went out to check the surroundings. The slopes above the village had been furrowed into ravines, and what used to be luxuriant fields was now utterly laid waste, with not an ear of grain left standing.

沒有。他感到絕望，只得再次呼喚神靈的名，痛哭流淚，摺起他的袍，用來鞭打土地。又大聲控訴家人所受到的虐待，及鄰居的罪行。

不久天上漸漸現出零散的雲朵，聚集成為一大片蓋頂的烏雲。突然電光閃爍，雷聲隆隆，雹暴爆發了！好像人間地獄，冰雹和雨水嘩啦嘩啦的傾倒着，又刮大風！米拉和達爾馬急忙跑回小屋躲避。

老婦人正在哭叫，不斷的捶着胸膛：「啊！我的收成完蛋了！我怎麼過這冬天啊？肯定會餓死啦！」

米拉簡直受不了，他不能殘酷這老婦人！他說：「用這片石把你的田畫在地板上。」她畫出一條狹窄的長方形，米拉連忙用自己的帽遮蓋着它，卻露出了尾部。雖然他這樣做對自己是有危險的，但他只想到要擋風遮雨。

當暴風雨過後，他們出去察看周圍的情況。村子上的斜坡都被犁成山溝。本來是肥沃的田地全毀了，不餘一杆

Surprisingly, one small strip of land at the edge of the village had kept its golden harvest! This was the old woman's field, which had been protected by Mila. Just one corner, not covered by his hat, was devastated by the storm and flooded with water. The old woman raised a cry of joy at first, and knelt down to thank the deities. After a while, when she had had time to reflect, she turned coldly to confront Mila. "You are Mila Thopaga, and you have destroyed this beautiful harvest. You are evil – leave my house at once!"

After Mila and Darma packed their belongings and left the cottage, the old woman swept the floor and went to the front door to spit at their backs.

As evening was approaching, Mila and Darma found shelter in a rock cave. They gathered some stunted shrubs and made a fire, and were busy warming themselves when they heard men's voices coming near. This was a party that had left the village at dawn to go hunting for game for the harvest celebrations. Detained by the storm, they were now on their way home, saying, "This Thopaga is a plague on us all! So many people have been killed, and now he has destroyed our beautiful harvest. If he fell into our hands at this moment, we'd cut him into pieces and share between us his flesh and his blood, drop by drop. Even that wouldn't be enough!"

As they passed in front of the cave, one of them said, "Keep

麥穗！出人意料的是：村邊一小片田地還有金黃色的收穫！

這是老婦人的田地，全靠米拉保存下來，但是沒被帽子遮蓋

的一角，就被風暴摧毀，又水浸。老婦人開心得大叫又跪下

感謝神恩。過一會兒，當她有時間反思時，她冷冷的面對米

拉：「你是米拉特巴加！就是你催毀了這美麗的豐收，你是

邪惡的一馬上滾出我的房子！」

當米拉和達爾馬收拾好行李離去時，老婦人立刻掃地並

向他們的背後吐口水！

天快黑了！米拉和達爾馬找到一岩洞棲身。他們收集了

一些柴枝，生起火取暖時，聽見有人走近。這幫人黎明離開

村子去打獵，想以獵物來慶祝豐收。他們被惡劣的天氣阻

擋，現在才回家。有人說：「這特巴加是我們的眼中釘，已

經殺了這麼多人，現在還毀了我們的豐收！如果他現在落在

我們手裏，我們要把他切碎，分攤他的肉，他的每滴血！就

是這樣也不足夠！」

當他們走過洞穴時，又有人說：「保持安靜、低聲！那

quiet, speak low! I see smoke over there. Who can be inside?"

"It must be Thopaga," another said. "Surely he can't have seen us yet. Let's hurry back to the village and bring up more men. We'll surround and kill him before he can do us more harm."

Mila and Darma watched them run back to the village. Darma said, "You'd better leave first. I'll stay here and wait for them. I'll impersonate you and lead them on a wild goose chase."

裏冒着煙，誰會在裏面？」

　　另一個人說：「一定是<u>特巴加</u>！他不會見到我們吧？我們馬上趕回去，多帶人來，包圍他，我們必要在他再來傷害我們之前，把他幹掉！」

　　<u>米拉</u>和<u>達爾馬</u>看着他們跑回去。<u>達爾馬</u>說：「你最好先離開，我留在這裏等他們。我假扮成你，引他們白費力氣追趕我！」

Chapter 16

SIN AND REPENTANCE

Mila knew Darma was a powerful fighter and a fast runner so had no misgivings about leaving him behind to deal with the villagers. He gave Darma a small bag filled with coarse sand and pebbles and said, "If they get too close, throw this at them to cast a spell."

After seeing Mila off, Darma left the cave to find a look-out position and saw small groups of men stealing forward from all directions to surround the cave. When they were near enough, he suddenly stood up, fully visible in the moonlight, and laughed out loud. "I am here!" He then raced downhill while the villagers had to climb uphill to catch him.

Darma had no problem out-distancing his pursuers. Whenever they fell too far behind, he slowed his steps so they could catch up. From time to time he taunted them. "Come on, you weaklings, catch me if you dare! You are only fit to fight women and children!" They ran on for hours, until finally Darma judged that Mila had had sufficient time to get away. He turned around to confront the villagers. "I've destroyed your harvest, and I can destroy all of you just as easily! Whoever makes the first move, I will kill him immediately and then his entire family."

第十六章
悔罪

米拉知道達爾馬善於打鬥又跑得很快,毫不猶疑地把他留下對付村人。他交給達爾馬一小袋粗沙和卵石,說:「如果他們迫近,你就把這些拋向他們下魔咒!」

達爾馬送走米拉後就離開洞穴,找到一個觀望點。他看見村人分成幾個小組,從不同方向靜靜地向山洞包抄。當他們靠近時,他突然站起來,月光照着他清晰可見!他大笑幾聲:「我在這裏!」然後他疾奔下山坡,村人卻要跑上山去追趕他!

達爾馬要拋離追逐他的人是毫無困難!每當他們落後太遠,他就會放緩腳步引他們追過來。他不時說話嘲弄他們:「有膽就來吧!你們這些頹弱的人來抓我吧!你們只配跟婦女和小孩打架!」他們不斷追逐數小時,等到達爾馬認為米拉有足夠時間脫身了,他轉過身來面對村人:「我摧毀了你們的收穫,我還能夠輕易的取你們所有人的性命!誰先向前一步,我就立即殺了他!然後殺他的一家。」

The villagers halted, looked at each other in tacit agreement, and then together they rushed at their enemy. Darma emptied the bag and threw the sand and pebbles at them, threatening, "You there, I see that you are the leader. Take one more step and you are dead." The man singled out hesitated and stopped, and the others stopped, too. Obviously the spell was taking effect, for they started to argue among themselves and then a fight broke out.

Before leaving them, Darma had the last word. "Make sure that you treat my mother and sister with respect and kindness, otherwise I'll wipe out your entire village!" He travelled on and stopped at the next town, where he found a wedding feast. After refreshing himself with food and drink and a good night's rest, he returned cheerfully to his Guru.

Mila didn't head in the opposite direction to get away, as expected. He wanted so much to see his mother and sister and, as most of his enemies were chasing Darma, he thought he could risk going back to the village. Avoiding the main road, he crept along behind rocks and bushes and felt his heart pounding as he neared home. Suddenly the dogs started barking and snarling. He had been away for so long that the dogs didn't recognise him anymore. He entered the village anyway, and a big dog attacked him and bit him on the leg, with the others ready to join in the fray. He fought off the dogs and, fortunately, the villagers had

村人停下來，彼此交換默契的眼色，然後一湧衝向敵人。達爾馬掏出袋子裏的砂石拋向他們，威脅的說：「你那裏，我看你是一個帶頭的！再走前一步你就死！」那個被挑選的人猶疑着停下，其餘的人也停步。魔咒顯靈了：他們吵起來又開始打鬥！

在離開前，達爾馬還要說幾句話：「你們保證要對我媽媽和妹妹友好和尊重！不然我就消滅這村子。」他繼續行程，停留在一個小鎮，那裏正舉行婚宴，有豐富的飲食和一夜酣睡，使他精神煥發，高興地回去永敦巴處。

出乎意料，米拉並沒有朝另一方向溜走，他渴望見到媽媽和妹妹。他想大概可以冒險回家，因為村裏多數人都在追捕達爾馬。他避開大路，一直躲在石頭和灌木後，快要到家了，他心跳得很厲害！狗突然狂吠，他離開太久，村狗已不認得他了。他不顧一切走進去，一頭大狗攻擊他，咬他的腿，其他狗也準備加入戰鬥。他打退了狗，幸而沒有驚動村人！

not been woken up by their noise. But Mila was forced to abandon his plan to see his mother and sister, and kept moving on.

Despite walking all night Mila was still not out of the area affected by the storm, because of his limp. At dawn he came to a mountain pasture and found a boy of about eleven years tending several wounded sheep. With tears in his eyes, the boy told Mila that they had lost their herds during the storm. His grandfather had gone searching for the surviving animals. Mila stayed with the boy and, when the old man returned carrying a lame goat on his shoulder, spent the whole morning helping them until they were sure all the surviving animals had been rounded up. When Mila left, he couldn't stop crying. The old shepherd looked so forlorn with his small grandson and their few straggly animals.

As he walked, Mila found several dead birds huddled together under a bramble bush, and others dead on the ground. He picked them up and put them in his cap, together with some dead rats. He even found a dead rabbit killed by the flood. When his cap and the lap of his robe were full, he dug a hole in the ground and buried the dead animals, shedding tears of remorse as he said the burial prayers, asking that they might have a better existence in the next life. He repeated this several times until he was out of the area affected by the storm. More and more, he was troubled by his heavy burden of sin, and deeply repented his

他被逼放棄回家探望媽媽和妹妹，只得繼續往前。

米拉一瘸一拐地走了一整夜，始終未走出被雹暴蹂躪的區域，黎明時他走到山上的草場，看到一個約十歲的牧童正在照料幾頭受傷的羊。牧童含淚告訴他：在暴風雨中他們失去了羊群，他的爺爺正在尋找倖存的動物。米拉陪着男孩等到老牧人背着跛腳的羊回來，他整個上午都在幫他們，直至找到所有倖存的牲口。米拉離開時不禁流淚，老人、小孩子和幾隻牲口，情況是多麼淒涼！

米拉一路走過去，他找到幾隻死鳥擠在黑莓灌木下，路上也有死鳥。他撿起牠們連同死老鼠一起放在帽子裏，他甚至發現淹死的兔子。當他的帽和袍的下擺都裝滿了死的動物，他在地上挖了個洞，埋葬牠們。他悔恨自責的流淚，給死去的動物唸超渡經文，祈求牠們下世輪迴能過好日子。他一再這樣做，直至走出風暴區域。他越來越受到罪惡感的困擾，他真心懺悔，不應利用黑魔法去降冰雹，傷害了這麼多

use of sorcery to produce the hailstorm that harmed so many. He yearned to see his guru and ask for advice.

He passed a village where he bought fresh provisions and then continued on his way. When evening approached, he found a sandstone cave to shelter in and, rather dispirited, went about gathering firewood in the vicinity. Suddenly a monkey jumped out of a bush nearby and seemed to charge at him. The monkey was riding a rabbit, wearing a mushroom for a helmet and carrying a long blade of straw for a spear. Mila was greatly astonished, and the spectacle was so ridiculous that he couldn't help laughing. The monkey charged past him and disappeared into the bush. Mila reflected, and then realised that he was being ridiculed; the Deities were laughing at him. He prostrated himself on the ground and cried miserably.

When he arrived at Yungtung's house, he knelt, tears streaming down his face. "Oh, Reverend Teacher, I begged you to teach me sorcery, but now I realise that I've heaped sin upon sin."

"Do not despair," Yungtung said. "All sentient beings, men or beast, possess a ray of the Eternal. I've learned from Holy Texts that all creatures killed by sorcery are in some manner saved, and attain a higher existence in their next life. I also know the ritual required, but it all depends on a true understanding of the Holy Doctrine. I'm not confident that my

人！他渴望見到他的導師，求他指點迷津。

他從經過的鄉村購買補給食品，又繼續他的行程。他找到一個沙岩洞過夜，有點沮喪，他到附近撿些柴火。忽然有一隻猴子從灌木叢跳出來，好像要衝向他！這猴子騎着大兔子，頭戴的蘑菇像頭盔，手執着麥稈帶着長葉片當作長矛！猴子衝過他旁邊又消失在叢木中。米拉大吃一驚，但如此荒謬的境像卻令他不禁笑起來。過了一會，米拉在反思，他意識到神靈正在嘲諷他荒謬的行為。他俯伏在地上，痛哭起來！

當他見到永敦巴時，他淚流滿面跪下：「敬愛的老師啊！我曾請求你傳授我巫術，但我現在明白了，我已經是罪上加罪！」

「你不必絕望！」永敦巴說：「凡是有知覺的生命，不論人或獸，都有靈性。我從經文得知：所有被巫術殺死的生命，反而會得救！下世輪迴會生在較高的層次。我亦知道所需要的儀式，可是這一切都全靠知道經文真正的意義。我

superficial knowledge can stand the test of the eternal."

"How can I learn this Holy Doctrine?" Mila asked.

"You'd have to devote your life to religious studies and work for the salvation of yourself and others," said Yungtung. "To seek the Holy Dharma is such a grave decision that it should only be made after fasting and the deep search of one's heart and soul."

Mila longed for redemption and forgiveness so much that he forgot to eat. He was filled with remorse and repentance. In the daytime when he was moving about, he wished that he was sitting down, but when he was sitting down, he wished that he was moving about. At night, he was unable to sleep. He continued to serve his guru, all the while yearning to go and learn the Holy Doctrine. He could not bring himself to ask for release, as the guru's wife had fallen seriously ill. Yungtung was nursing her night and day but soon after, she died. Yungtung was heartbroken with grief.

A few days after the funeral, Yungtung sent for Mila. "How transitory this life of ours is," he said sadly. "Yanchela has passed away and I mourn her deeply. It seems like only yesterday when she was so beautiful and everywhere about the house. Looking back, I realise the misery of my entire life. Ever since my youth, the black arts have been my whole career: dealing out death by sorcery and causing destruction through

只有膚淺的知識，沒信心經得起永恆的考驗！」

米拉說：「我怎樣才可學習這神聖的教義？」

永敦巴說：「你要把你的一生奉獻給宗教，又做拯救自己及他人的工作。想去修行悟道是非常重大的事，你必須齋戒及冥想，誠心作這決定。」

米拉渴望着被寬恕與救贖，他日夜不安以至廢寢忘餐！日間他在走動時，就想坐下來，當坐着他又想走動。到晚上他又無法入睡！他照舊為喇嘛服務，但他只想着去修行。他不忍要求喇嘛立刻釋放他，因為永敦巴的妻子正病重。他日夜不停照料她，但不久她去世了，永敦巴心碎了很悲痛！

葬禮過後數天，永敦巴派人去叫米拉，他說：「人生是如此短暫！賢切拉已經去世了，我深切懷念她！好像只是昨天她還是生氣勃勃，美麗活潑地滿屋走動！回想過去，我一生是多麼痛苦！從我年輕時，我就認定黑魔法是我的終身職業：施行巫術去殺人及降冰雹去摧毀。我兒啊！你年紀輕輕

hailstorms. My son, you too have devoted your young life to this sinful art and have already acquired a load of bad Karma. I also must carry your load, since I am responsible for what you've done."

With tears streaking his face, Mila said, "Oh, Reverend Teacher, this life is short. What can we do to prevent the fate of falling into hell, or being reborn into a lower state of being?"

"I now wish to devote my life to religion," Yungtung said, "and to find a true doctrine that will stand firm and solid against everything that threatens. If you remain here as guardian to my children and my disciples, I will go out and seek my salvation as well as yours. The other alternative is for you to go, to learn and practise the Holy Dharma on my behalf, as well as for yourself. This way, we can both achieve salvation so that in our next life, we can progress further along the Path of Emancipation. I will give you all the material support you need."

Mila was filled with great joy, for this was exactly his wish. He immediately begged for permission to take up the religious life, and Yungtung consented. "You are young and energetic. You are also richly endowed with faith, insight and perseverance. You will make a very good devotee. Go and live a life of pure religion."

He gave Mila a cow yak loaded with fine Yarlung woolen material, and directed him to search out a famous lama who

就致力於這種邪惡的法術，到目前已累積了很重的罪孽。我也要分擔你的罪孽，因為我要為你做的事負上責任。」

米拉淚流滿面說：「尊敬的老師啊！人生是如此短暫！我們要怎麼做才能免受地獄之苦，又不會再世沉淪為低等生物呢？」

永敦巴說：「我想出家修行，尋找至高無上的真理。如果你留在這裏做我的兒女和門徒的監護人，我就可以出家求道，讓我和你都得救！另一種解決方案，就是你出家去修行，為我亦為了你自己。這樣我們都得道，可以再世為人。你要走上這一條邁向解脫的大道，我會供給你物質上的支持。」

米拉高興極了，這正是他的願望。他立刻求永敦巴准許他出家去修行。永敦巴同意了：「你年輕精力充沛，有天賦、信心、毅力，又能堅持，你會是個好的修行者，你就獻身宗教吧！」

他供給米拉一頭母犁牛，滿載着上好的羊毛織料，又指示他去找一位著名的喇嘛，他是密宗又擁有超自然力量。

belonged to an old mystic sect and was known to have supernatural power.

Thus Yungtung sent his disciple forth to seek the Transcendental Truths and set the wheel of the dharma in motion. Mila did not waver in his life's pursuit, and meditated unceasingly for many years. After overcoming immense difficulties and with great sacrifice, he finally attained the highest of all spiritual knowledge, the Truth of Eternity.

永敦巴就這樣送他的門徒出家尋道，他推動了命運之輪。米拉從不動搖，他多年來不斷冥想，追求真理。他克服了極大的困難，又作出許多犧牲，他最終得道，在世成佛！歷代西藏人都崇拜他。

Chapter 17

EPILOGUE

Mila needed to find the right guru who could lead him on his path to true religion. He went to several teachers and finally, he was fortunate enough to be accepted as a *chela* (a disciple) by Marpa the Translator. Marpa had gone to India in his youth and brought back scripts of Gautama Buddha's teachings. Marpa's career was mainly in translating and teaching of the holy scripts. Mila studied and meditated under Marpa, and fired with religious zeal, vowed to Marpa that he would devote his whole life to religion and forsake all worldly connections.

Seven years went by, but one night Mila had a dream. He dreamt that he went home and found his house, the Four and Eight, had fallen completely into ruin. Part of the roof had caved in, all the doors and windows were missing, and grass was growing in the main living room. His mother was dead and his sister Peta was missing and could not be found. When he woke up, his face was wet with tears. He had such an irresistible yearning to see his mother and sister again that he decided to go to his Lama and ask for immediate release.

Mila found his teacher fast asleep in his bedroom, as it was still night time. Mila knelt beside the bed and waited. Marpa

第十七章
後記

米拉需要有名師帶領他修行才能找到正道，他跟隨過幾位導師，幸而他終於成為瑪爾巴大師的門徒。瑪爾巴年青時去過印度，帶回來釋迦牟尼的經文。至於他的事業，主要就是翻譯及傳授這些聖典。米拉在瑪爾巴門下修道令他充滿宗教熱情，他發誓出家要終身修行。

七年平靜的過去了，米拉一夜發了個夢，他夢見自己回到家裏。他家的房子有名的「四樑八柱」，已經完全荒廢。部份屋頂已經倒塌，所有門和板窗都失踪，而大廳的地板上長着草！他的媽媽已經過世，妹妹百德也失踪了，不知去向！他醒過來，滿臉都是淚。他有不可抗拒的渴望，要回家見他的媽媽和妹妹！他決定立刻去找喇嘛，請求他許可。

他找到瑪爾巴時，仍然是晚上，瑪爾巴正在他的臥室酣

woke when light streamed through the window and shone on his face. After hearing Mila's plea for release, Marpa bowed his head in deep thought and said, "My son, I can see there's no stopping you! You must go home, although when you first came, you did vow to give up all worldly connections. I've read the omens and can foretell that we'll not meet again in this life. I prophesize that you'll be a great one in our religion, for when I first woke up, I saw light on your head, like a halo!"

After three days' ritual of prayer and meditation, Mila was allowed to leave. He was deeply grateful to Marpa and vowed that he'd never stray from his chosen path of religion.

Knowing that he was hated by the villagers, Mila was cautious and did not go home directly. He stopped at a mountain pasture overlooking his village. Pretending to be a traveler passing by, he talked casually with a young shepherd. Pointing to this house and that, he asked about the occupants, and then pointing at his own house he asked, "Who lives in that big house?"

"It's a haunted house; nobody lives there," the boy said.

"Oh, tell me about it!" Mila said

The boy said, "A wealthy family used to live there, but when the head of the family died, the uncle and aunt took all the property and left the widow destitute with her son and daughter. The only son became a sorcerer and used black magic to take

睡，<u>米拉</u>跪在牀邊等候着。當曙光穿過窗戶照在<u>瑪爾巴</u>的臉然後說：「我兒，我知道現在無法阻止你，你一定要回家！雖然你初到時，你曾經發誓出家。我已看到預兆，知道我們今生不會再見面！我現在預言你會是我教中的偉大人物！當我醒來時，我看見晨光照着你的頭頂，你像戴上了光環！」他們齋戒祈禱了三天，然後才讓<u>米拉</u>離開寺院，<u>米拉</u>深深感謝<u>瑪爾巴</u>，他發誓不會還俗，永遠出家修行。

<u>米拉</u>明知村人痛恨他，所以不敢直接回家，他在山上的草原歇息，俯瞰着村子，他假裝是旅客和那牧童聊天：「誰住在那大房子？」

孩子說：「那是鬼屋沒人住在那裏。」

<u>米拉</u>說：「告訴我吧！」

孩子說：「那曾經是有錢人的家，當屋主死後，伯父和姑母搶奪了所有財產，寡婦和孤兒陷入貧困。那獨子走出去學法術，他變成巫師用黑魔法報復，殺了村裏不少人，後來

revenge on his Uncle and Aunt, killing a lot of people in this village. Later he also brought down a hailstorm that destroyed the year's crop of the entire village. That house is spooked! Although it all happened many years ago, we are still afraid of the sorcerer. People don't go near the house and we don't even look in that direction."

"What happened to the mother and daughter?" Mila asked.

"About five years ago, the mother died suddenly," the boy said. "Her daughter immediately ran off, leaving the mother's dead body still in that house. The daughter has completely disappeared from the village. It's really shocking!"

Mila felt his heart was broken and immediately headed for his old home. He found the house in ruins exactly as it had appeared in his dream. When he was going through the empty rooms, he noticed on the floor of the main living room a pile of old rags and dirt with luxuriant grass growing over it. On closer examination, he found a skeleton and realized that it was the remains of his mother. Mila collapsed with unbearable anguish, and fell down to embrace his dead mother.

He lay there with the heap of bones the whole night in black despair until he remembered his guru's teachings. He then meditated and was able to commune spiritually with his mother. He remained in deep meditation for seven days and communed with the spirits of both of his parents. He was able to help them

他又降雹暴，摧毀了整村的收獲！那房子有鬼！雖然已是多年前的事，我們仍然害怕巫師，大家都不敢走近房子，我們甚至不敢往那方向瞧！」

米拉問：「後來那兩母女又怎樣？」

孩子說：「大約五年前，母親猝然死去！她的女兒立刻逃走，留下母親的屍體不管，現在仍然在那房子裏，女兒從此不再見。多麼可怕，真是令人震驚！」

米拉心都碎了，馬上打道回家。他發現荒廢的房子正如他夢中所見，當他走過那些空房間時，他看見大廳地板上有一堆破布和污垢，上面長着青綠的草。他仔細看，發現了屍骨，然後知道這就是他母親的遺體！難忍的痛苦令他崩潰了，他倒下去擁抱死去的母親。

他整夜和那堆骸骨躺在一起，感到漆黑的絕望！他終於記起喇嘛的教誨，開始打坐冥想，直至他能與母親的靈魂溝通。接着坐禪七天，這期間他與父母的靈魂溝通，幫助他們

move towards their next lives. When he finally rose, he realized that all his worldly ties were cut and henceforth, he could live a life of pure religion. He also knew that he'd meet with his sister Peta again in the near future, and that she was also destined for a religious life.

He wanted to give his mother the accepted burial, but for that, he needed the help of the village Lama. He gathered up his mother's bones and brought them to his old tutor, Lama Lugyat-Khan at the Invisible Knoll School. He also brought as payment a set of holy books bound in thick leather, the only valuable things left in the house. Mila was surprised to find that Lama Lugyat-Khan had passed away and that his son Chudor had taken over as schoolmaster. Lama Chudor remembered Mila and cordially invited him to stay for a few days. Lama Chudor also offered to help without any payment, but Mila insisted on his gift of the set of holy books.

According to custom, the bones were first pulverized into powder and mixed with clay and then molded into miniature *stupas* (burial mounds). On parting, Chudor gave Mila the *stupas* and advised," You can come home safely. The villagers are in awe of your black magic and won't do you harm. You should marry Zesay and rebuild your house. I think you can have a large following as a lama."

Mila just smiled and said, "I cannot live a worldly life. This

輪迴，再世投胎。當他站起來，他清楚知道自己不再有塵世的牽掛，一生都可以投入宗教了。他又知道很快就會和妹妹見面，她也是命中注定要出家修行的。

他想按照俗例下葬母親，因此他需要村喇嘛的幫助。他把骸骨收拾好，把它帶到隱形山學校，他以前的老師那裏。他把一套皮革釘裝的聖經帶去作酬勞，那是家裏唯一的貴重物品。想不到米拉的導師已過世！現在他的兒子卓多爾喇嘛是校長。卓多爾認識米拉就誠邀他停留數天，卓多爾又願意免費服務，但米拉堅持要送他那套聖經。

習俗是把骸骨磨成粉和粘土混合製造成小塔。臨別時，卓多爾把塔子交給米拉說：「你搬來住不會有危險，村人都敬畏你的法術，不敢與你敵對。你應該和澤思結婚，重建你的家園，我認為你當喇嘛會有很多信徒。」

米拉只微笑說：「我不能過世俗的生活，生命是短暫的，

life is short, and I must cling to solitude and work for enlightenment, to achieve the wisdom of the eternity, so that I can be released from the bonds of the Wheel of Transmigration." Chudor gave Mila a bag of flour and a roll of butter as provisions and saw him off. Mila found a small rock cave in a mountain slope nearby, where he deposited his mother's bones. After performing the burial ritual for her, he sealed the cave.

Mila's final act was to travel into the wilderness and begin a life of prayer and meditation, emerging on rare occasions only to beg for the necessary provisions. However, people gradually came to hear of this great prophet and some went into the wilderness to follow him. His reputation grew throughout his life and eventually he had thousands of followers.

我必須獨自修行尋求永生。」卓多爾給米拉一袋麵粉和牛油，就道別了。米拉在附近山上找到一小岩洞，他把母親的遺體放進去，親自唸誦經文，然後把洞穴密封。

最後米拉進入荒野，過着獨自修行的生活，他只是偶爾出來求人布施，然而世人漸漸得知他是偉大的先知！亦有人走到荒野追隨他，他的一生越來越著名，後來他的門徒數以千計。

Appendix A

The Tibetan Bonn Sect

Bonn originated from the traditional beliefs of the tribes of the time and is the oldest religion in Tibet. As a formal religion, it was founded in the fifth Century BC by a Tibetan prince and was believed in by all the tribes in every part of Tibet until the arrival of Buddhism in the seventh century AD. Buddhism came from India and struggled with the Bonn Sect's influence for over a thousand years, when Buddhism became predominant. However, Bonn is still worshipped today by over a million followers, with approximately 3000 monks in 100 monasteries.

Bonn is mainly about nature worship: the sun, the moon, stars, mountains, rocks, trees, streams, lakes, cattle, sheep, wild animals, etc. The deities and spirits are categorised as heavenly deities, earthly spirits and spirits from the underworld. The Bonn Lama is a leading social figure, as he has to be consulted about all important events, such as marriage, burial, planting, harvest and the naming of babies.

During the long struggle between Bonn and Buddhism, the two religions became assimilated adapting to each other in many ways. To survive, Bonn has adopted some Buddhist theory and ceremony, while Buddhism took on many Bonn practices to

附錄一

西藏波恩教派

波恩教起源於西藏部落的傳統信仰，是最古老的宗教。在公元前五世紀，一位西藏王子正式成立了波恩教，波恩教曾經是整個西藏，所有部落的信仰，直至七世紀佛教從印度傳過來，二派競爭超過一千年，然後佛教成為西藏的主要宗教。目前，波恩教在西藏仍然有一百萬信徒，大約三千僧人和一百座廟宇。

波恩教主要是崇拜自然：太陽、月亮、星星、山、岩石、樹木、溪流、湖泊、牛、羊、野生動物等。波恩神靈分為三種分類，就是天神、地仙和地獄的鬼怪。波恩喇嘛是社會領袖，重要的事就要徵詢他的意見，例如：婚姻、埋葬、種植、收獲、嬰兒命名等。波恩與佛教的長期鬥爭令到兩教同化，多方面互相適應。波恩教採用了一些佛教的理論和儀式，而

adapt to local customs. Followers of both religions pray by turning a prayer wheel and moving beads along a string, but they do this in opposite directions. The Buddhist monastery is headed by a living Buddha who is reborn from generation to generation, while the Bonn chief Lama fills a hereditary position. Bonn is known as the black sect, as its followers wear a black head-scarf.

佛教為了要本地化，沿用了很多<u>波恩</u>教的慣例。兩教的信徒祈禱時都轉動祈禱輪和用一串唸珠，但他們沿用相反的方向去轉輪。佛教寺廟的首領是轉世活佛，而領導<u>波恩</u>寺廟的喇嘛是世襲的。<u>波恩</u>教通常被稱為黑教，因為信徒都戴黑頭巾。

Appendix B

Factions in Tibetan Buddhism

There are four major factions in Tibetan Buddhism: the White Sect (Kagyu), the Red Sect (Nyngma), the Flower Sect (Sakya) and the Yellow Sect (Gelug).

The White Sect (Kagyu)

The White Sect is distinctive in its oral tradition. The religion is passed on individually from teacher to selected pupils. It is commonly known as the White Sect because the lamas wear white following the Indian tradition. The emphasis is on severe practice rather than theory. Consequently, this sect is known for the great lamas like Milarepa, both hermit and ascetic.

This sect flourished during the Ming Dynasty and its head was appointed as the royal priest by the Ming Emperor in 1413 A.D. He was honoured with the title "Karmapa" which still applies today. The succession of the Karmapa is through reincarnation. In Tibetan history, the White Sect is the first to introduce this system of succession.

The Red Sect (Nyngma)

The Red Sect is the oldest faction in Tibetan Buddhism. It

附錄二

藏傳佛教的派別

藏傳佛教主要有四大派別：噶舉派（白教）、寧瑪派（紅教）、薩迦派（花教）及格魯派（黃教）

噶舉派（白教）

噶舉派可理解為口傳宗派。僧人按印度傳統穿白袍，俗稱「白教」，由馬爾巴創立。特色是不重著述而重視實際的修行，強調刻苦的修行，造就了如米拉日巴等眾多苦行修煉的高僧。

在明朝此教最為興盛，明成祖（公元 1413 年）冊封法王為國師，號稱「大寶法王」，正名是「大寶法王噶瑪巴」，藏人直接尊稱為「噶瑪巴」，承傳至今。法王的繼承方式是轉世，為西藏歷史上最早實行轉世制度的宗派。

寧瑪派（紅教）

寧瑪派是藏傳佛教最古老的派別，它是最早傳入西藏的密教

originally came from India and has absorbed some elements from the native Bonn Sect. It is commonly known as the Red Sect because the lamas wear a red hat.

The Nyngma lamas fall mainly into two categories. Those belonging to the first category, commonly called "Ah Pa", perform a religious role in society by reciting prayers and incantations, blessings and curses, soothsaying, etc. They are not theorists and have little knowledge of Buddhist teachings. Those in the second category have books and pass on their beliefs from teacher to pupil, or from father to son. In some places, the lamas are not strictly organized and they can marry and have a family.

In times of war, natural disasters or plague, it has always been the custom through the ages for the Tibetan government to appoint the Red Sect lamas to perform rites in public. They are recognized by society at large as high priests, prophets and soothsayers. The Red Sect is popular not only in Tibet but has also spread to other countries like: India, Nepal, France, the United States of America, etc.

The Flower Sect (Sakya)

There are stripes in red, white and black, representing the three Buddha, painted on the exterior walls of the main Sakya Temple, and therefore it is commonly called the Flower Sect. This faction was founded by Tibetan nobility and with the support of

並吸收了原始苯教的一些內容。由於該派僧人戴紅色帽，俗稱「紅教」。

寧瑪派僧人可分兩大類：第一類稱阿巴，專靠念經念呪在社會活動，不注重學習佛經，也無佛教理論。第二類有經典，也有師徒或父子間傳授，某些地方對僧侶要求不甚嚴格可娶妻生子。

歷屆西藏政府每逢戰爭、天災、瘟疫等，都要請寧瑪派僧人作法禳解，寧瑪高僧一直都被社會接納為祈禱師，負責占卜問卦。如今紅教不僅流傳在西藏，已經廣為傳播至印度、尼泊爾、美國、法國等地。

薩迦派（花教）

薩迦派的主寺——薩迦寺圍牆塗有紅、白、黑三色花條，象徵三位菩薩，故俗稱「花教」。此教由西藏貴族「昆氏」家族建立與發展。西元 13 世紀中，得到元朝的支持成為有強大政治勢力的教派，為元朝統一西藏作出了重要的貢獻，法王

the Yuen Dynasty, it became very powerful politically in the 13th Century A.D. It had helped the Yuen dynasty to gain the overall control of Tibet. Kublai Khan appointed its head to be his royal priest and the Flower Sect ruled Tibet completely until the 14th Century A.D. Its influence went into decline with the rise of the White Sect.

The head of the Sect, the Dharma King, has the honorific "Mahayana" and succession is by blood. The first born of two noble families alternatively succeed to the throne of "Mahayana".

The Flower Sect has made important contributions towards Tibetan culture. During the Yuen Dynasty, the Mahayana invited experts from China, Tibet and India to Beijing and they spent three years in compiling the Buddhist Bible, the Tripitaka. The Sakya Temple has the largest collection of Buddhist books and manuscripts. It is also the most famous Buddhist printing press for the publication of books on religion, medicine, the Tibetan calendar, etc.

The Yellow Sect (Gelug)

The Tibetan word "gelug" means discipline, therefore this sect is known for its strict discipline. It is commonly known as the Yellow Sect because the lamas wear a yellow hat. It is the most recent sect, as it became popular only in the 15th Century A.D.,

被元世祖忽必烈封為國師。此教曾掌握了西藏政教的全權，

至西元 14 世紀噶舉派興起而漸取代，薩迦派漸衰退。薩迦派

法王稱為「大乘法王」世襲繼承。歷來由二大王族的長子輪

流掌法王之位。

　　薩迦派對西藏文化有重要的貢獻，此教法王在元代曾召

集藏、漢及印度名僧到北京，歷時三年撰成「藏文大藏經」。

　　薩迦寺是藏佛經，典最豐富的寺院，也是最著名的印經

院，專門刻印佛經、曆法、醫學等多種典籍。對於保存和弘

揚佛教有很大的作用。

格魯派（黃教）

藏語「格魯」即善律，該派嚴守戒律，僧人戴黃色帽故又名

黃教。格魯派是藏傳佛教中最後興起的，在西元 15 世紀才

but it soon overtook all the others. It has become the most influential faction in Tibetan society. It has assimilated the teachings and experience of the other, earlier factions and therefore was better organized. Its teachings value both theory and practice and it has a good system of managing the temples. The lamas have to pass strict examinations, remain celibate, keep discipline and refrain from labour.

Its head was officially appointed by the Ming Dynasty in the 15th Century A.D. and the Qing Dynasty further confirmed the two separate systems of succession: one for the Da Lai Lama and one for the Banchan Lama.

The Yellow Sect became the ruling party and the union of church and state was further developed in Tibet.

興起。它迅速取代了其他各教派的地位，在西藏社會成為最重要的教派，影響很大。由於最晚出現，它汲取了以前各宗派的教法，學修並重，有完善寺院管理制度，僧人要通過嚴格的考試，守戒律，不事農務，獨身不娶。

格魯派的法王在西元 15 世紀曾受明廷冊封，至清代該派的達賴與班禪兩轉世系統均由清廷確認，格魯派成為西藏的執政教派，進一步發展政教合一的統治形式。

Note from the Author

I was born and grew up in Hong Kong and have the advantage of bilingual education. When I worked as a translator of literature, mainly from English to Chinese, I met many famous writers and poets. The Canadian poet Michael Bullock asked me to translate his work. His book "The Walled Garden", translated by me, was published in Kwangsi, China in 1998 (with a grant from the Canada Council). The book was a sold-out success. I have also won prizes for translation in Taiwan (梁實秋文學翻譯獎) for two years.

I was first encouraged to write by Professor Yu Kuang Chung (余光中教授). Many of my poems were published in the "Blue Star" (藍星詩刊), a well-known poetry magazine of Taiwan, edited by Professor Yu. Mr. Liu Yi Chang (劉以鬯), the famous novelist and editor, also encouraged me by publishing my poems and short stories in his magazine "Hong Kong Literature" (香港文學). I have also published short stories, poems and articles in Hong Kong newspapers. Some of my work is collected in the Hong Kong Central Library, Hong Kong Literature Room (http://hkclweb.hkpl.gov.hk), under my pen name Zhang Jian (章簡).

I began to take a serious look into Buddhism several years. Brought up under the British Colonial system, I was educated in a Christian high school and then took a B.A. in English Literature at the University of London. My sincere desire to investigate my own cultural background is understandable. I must admit that Buddhist thinking has influenced me: I am more in touch with my own subconscious. I feel more in control of myself, and therefore, of my world. Although I am mainly interested in Chinese Buddhism (Zen), I also find Tibetan Buddhism very intriguing. When I came to read about Milarepa, I was fascinated and started to write my own story of the great Yogi. The result is my new book, "Mila the Magician".

Zhang Jian 章簡
Hong Kong 2013

關於我的種種

我原名羅章蘭，筆名章簡，籍貫廣西。在香港出生、成長，中學階段的中、英雙語教育令我得益匪淺。後來我從事翻譯，在文學圈子裏，認識到不少作家。在 90 年代我們全家移居加拿大溫哥華。當地的著名詩人布邁格請我翻譯他的詩集，結果 1988 年我翻譯的布邁格詩集《牆內花園》在廣西出版（由加拿大文化協會贊助）。這本雙語書在中國大陸相當受歡迎，一千多本全部售罄。數年後我們全家回香港居住。我亦曾兩度得台灣的梁實秋翻譯獎。

我從開始寫作時，得到余光中教授的鼓勵，我的詩作發表在他主編的《藍星詩刊》。亦得到著名作家劉以鬯先生的鼓勵，在他主編的《香港文學》經常發表我的詩、散文和短篇小說。我的作品在香港的各報刊發表，部份作品收錄在香港中央圖書館[1]。

近年來我認真的去探討佛教。我成長於殖民地社會，就讀於基督教中學，然後在倫敦大學唸英國文學。這洋化的背景反而令我渴望認識中國的文化和傳統。我必須承認佛教對我的影響！我比以前更能觸摸到自己的潛意識，更在自己的控制中，因此而有我的世界。我主要對中國禪宗感興趣，但我覺得藏傳佛教最耐人尋味！當我閱讀到米拉日巴的傳說，我被迷住了。我開始寫關於這位偉大瑜伽大師的故事，結果是我的新書《魔劫》。

章簡
2013 年香港

---

[1] 參見 http://hkclweb.hkpl.gov.hk（筆名：章簡）

Lomen

Lomen is a Taiwan Poet who has been prolific for over half a century and has achieved a great reputation. Over one million words of criticism have been written about his poems by critics both in Taiwan and abroad, and numerous doctoral dissertations have discussed his work. He is well known internationally and is listed in "The Poets Dictionary in the World" and "Encyclopaedia Americana".

His writing covers a wide range of subjects. Main themes of his poetry are war and death and in search of the human spirit. He was awarded the Gold Medal by the President of the Philippines in 1966 for his famous poem, 'Fort Mckinly', which deals with the memorial cemetery, built in the suburbs of Manila by the United States Government to commemorate the sixty thousand soldiers who died in the Pacific Region during the Second World War. This poem has been cited as a great contemporary work by the Chairman at the World Congress of Poets.

Lomen has also written literary theory and art criticism. He emphasizes that poetry is a synthesis of beauty and spirituality. At present he is still very active in literary circles in Taiwan, where he is variously acclaimed as "Taiwan's Apollinaire", "the Father of Urban Poetry", "War Poet", etc. He has judged literary prizes in Taiwan and has also been Chairman of the World Chinese Poets Society. To celebrate the 200th anniversary of the U.S.A., the World Conference of Poets was held in Washington in 1976. As guests of honour, Lomen and his wife Rongzi (also a well-known poet) were both crowned as poet laureates.

Lomen is an important art critic and pioneered installation art in Taiwan. He has built a "House of Lights" in Taipei and another in Hainan. The "houses" are for the permanent exhibition of installation art and serve as good illustrations of his concepts of art and beauty.

羅門簡介

羅門是台灣著名詩人，從事詩創作超半世紀，作品甚豐，成就巨大。國內、外的學者評論他的作品超 100 萬字。已出版 7 本評論羅門的書，又有多篇研究羅門的碩士、博士論文。他擁有國際聲望，名列《世界詩人辭典》及《大美百科全書》。

羅門作品的題材廣闊，致力於心靈的探索。他的代表詩作《麥堅利堡》於 1966 年獲菲律賓總統金牌獎，同時此詩曾在「國際詩人大會」中，被主席宣稱為近代偉大的詩作。

羅門除寫詩，尚寫詩論與藝評，有「台灣阿波里奈爾」與「台灣現代裝置藝術[2]鼻祖」之稱。此外羅門曾任國家文藝獎評審委員、世界華文詩人協會會長以及更被名評論家在文章中稱為：「重量級詩人」、「戰爭詩的巨擘」、「都市詩之父」、「大師級詩人」、「詩人中的詩人」。1976 年值美國建國 200 周年紀念，在美國華盛頓舉行數十個國家的世界詩人大會，羅門、蓉子[3]應邀以貴賓出席此次大會，夫婦接受加冕頒為桂冠詩人。

---

[2] 裝置藝術——英文稱為「Installation Art」
[3] 蓉子——台灣著名詩人

Yu Kuang Chung

Professor Yu Kuang Chung is a prominent man of letters. He has taught in universities in Taiwan, Hong Kong, Mainland China and also in the U.S.A. At present, he is Professor Emeritus at Zhongshan University, Kaohsiung, Taiwan, where he was for six years Dean of the Faculty of Arts.

Many of Professor Yu's published works have been acclaimed, including poetry collections, essays, literary criticism and translations of plays and fiction. He has published over fifty different books and has been active in the literary world for over half a century. In Taiwan, he has been awarded all the important literary prizes. In Hong Kong, he is widely known, because, for example, he has taught at the Chinese University of Hong Kong, won the Henry Fok Prize for Achievement and the Best Book of the Year Prize, among others.

Recently in China, CCTV broadcast a series of programmes to cover Professor Yu's life and work. A film was made in Hong Kong based on his poem, "The Pearl Necklace". A film documentary series, "They Write Poems on this Island", including a programme on Professor Yu, has been shown in Hong Kong. His famous poem, Home Sickness', has become widely known throughout the Chinese-speaking world. Some of his essays, such as "Listen to the Cold Rain" and "My Four Imaginary Enemies", have been chosen as study texts for students in Mainland China, Hong Kong and Taiwan. As a contemporary writer, Yu Kuang Chung is a household name.

Professor Yu is also known internationally. Many years ago, by invitation of the U.S. Department of State, Professor Yu was guest lecturer at a number of U.S. universities. Many of his works have been translated and published abroad. He has frequently attended conferences organized by PEN and other literary conferences in the U.S.A. and Europe. He is included in the *Encyclopedia of World Literature in the Twentieth Century*, New York, 1993.

余光中簡介

余光中為當代著名文學家。他一直都在各地大學任教，包括台灣、香港、祖國大陸及海外。自 1985 年至今在台灣高雄市中山大學任講座教授，其間擔任文學院院長六年。

　　余光中的著作甚豐，現已出版的詩集、散文集、評論集、翻譯集多達五十餘種。至今馳騁文壇已逾半世紀，所得的獎項包括台灣所有重要的文學獎。他也是香港人熟悉的作家，曾在香港中文大學任教，得到霍英東成就獎、香港年度十大好書等獎項。

　　近年來中央電視台的專題節目連續推薦，報道余光中。1998 年，他的詩作《珍珠項鍊》在香港被拍為影片。2011 年電影《他們在島嶼寫詩》，其中有余光中專輯。其詩作《鄉愁》傳遍華語世界。散文如《聽聽那冷雨》、《我的四個假想敵》等，都被收進兩岸的教科書。余光中已是深入人心的當代文學家。

　　余光中多年前應美國國務院邀請，曾赴美多家大學任客座教授。他曾多次赴歐、美參加國際筆會及其他文學會議，並發表演講。1993 年，余光中被納入《二十世紀文學大全》。

In recent years, Professor Yu has frequently given speeches and lectured in Mainland China. In 2012, he was Poet-in-Residence at Beijing University. At present, he is continuing his "Tug-of-War with Immortality",[5] alive and well, but has already become a part of history. His name shows up prominently in the annals of modern Chinese Literature.

　　近年來，<u>余光中</u>多次到大陸講學，在 2012 年應<u>北京大學</u>邀請，任駐校詩人。他目前仍在《與永恆拔河》[4]。生活在當今卻已經進入了歷史，名字顯目地刻在現代<u>中國</u>文學的史冊上。

---

[4] 註：<u>余光中</u>詩集《與永恆拔河》1979 年出版

NOTES

[1] "Lama" means, "monk"; "guru" means "teacher", and "yogi" is a practitioner of yoga. Yoga was originally the most important spiritual practice in Buddhism; however it has been popularized and has gradually changed with use over many years.

[2] Please see Appendix, "Tibetan Bonn Sect".

[3] According to common Tibetan etiquette, a *hada* (a long narrow woven scarf that varies in length from 1 metre to 10 metres) is presented to show respect at most social occasions, e.g. a wedding, a funeral, going to the temple, receiving a guest, saying farewell, etc. Hadas are usually white in colour, to signify good luck and purity.

[4] Dakinis can be compared to elves, angels and such supernatural beings. The word "dakinis" means sky dancers. They are traditionally depicted as beautiful, naked women with a volatile temperament, usually wrathful. They serve as messengers and inspirers from the gods to human beings, but sometimes they act as temptresses and tricksters. Dakinis are poetic beings who can lead us to spirituality. However, Dakinis are spirits who have not yet achieved the eternal life of a god. A dakini could have been a lama in the previous life, and in the next life, could go higher or lower, according to the Wheel of Transmigration.

[5] "Tug-of-War with Immortality" is the name of a poetry collection by Professor Yu Kuang Chung published in 1979.

ABOUT PROVERSE HONG KONG

Proverse Hong Kong is based in Hong Kong with strong regional and international connections.

Proverse has published novels, novellas, non-fiction (including fictionalized autobiography and biography, autobiography, biography, history, memoirs, sport, travel narratives), single-author poetry collections, young teens and academic books. Other interests include diaries, and academic works in the humanities, social sciences, cultural studies, linguistics and education. Some Proverse books have accompanying audio texts. Some are translated into Chinese.

Proverse welcomes authors who have a story to tell, wisdom, perceptions or information to convey, a person they want to memorialize, a neglect they want to remedy, a record they want to correct, a strong interest that they want to share, skills they want to teach, and who consciously seek to make a contribution to society in an informative, interesting and well-written way. Proverse works with texts by non-native-speaker writers of English as well as by native English-speaking writers.

The name, "Proverse", combines the words "prose" and "verse" and is pronounced accordingly.

THE PROVERSE PRIZE

The Proverse Prize, an annual international competition for an unpublished, publishable, single-author book-length work of fiction, non-fiction, or poetry, the original work of the entrant, submitted in English (translations welcomed) was established in January 2008. It is open to all who are at least eighteen on the date they sign the entry form and without restriction of nationality, residence or citizenship.

Its objectives are: to encourage excellence and / or excellence and usefulness in publishable written work in the English Language, which can, in varying degrees, "delight and instruct". Entries are invited from anywhere in the world.

The Prize
1) Publication by Proverse Hong Kong, with
2) Cash prize of HKD10,000 (HKD7.80 = approximately USD1.00)

Extent of the Manuscript: within the range of what is usual for the genre of the work submitted. However, it is advisable that novellas be in the range, 35,000 to 50,000 words; other fiction (e.g. novels, short-story collections) and non-fiction (e.g. autobiographies, biographies, diaries, letters, memoirs, essay collections, etc.) should be in the range, 80,000 to 110,000 words. Poetry collections should be in the range, 8,000 to 30,000 words. Other word-counts and mixed-genre submissions are not ruled out.

Annual Entry Deadlines
(subject to confirmation and/or change)

Receipt of Entry Fees/ Entry Forms begins	14 April
Deadline for receipt of Entry Fees / Entry Forms	31 May
Receipt of entered manuscripts begins	1 May
Deadline for receipt of entered manuscripts	30 June

More information, updated from time to time, is available on the Proverse website: proversepublishing.com

Those who enjoy "Mila The Magician" may also enjoy the following books published by Proverse

ASTRA AND SEBASTIAN: AN EPIC LOVE STORY by L.W. Illsley. HK & UK, November 2011. Pbk. Illustrated by Shelley Knowles-Dixon. Proverse Prize Finalist (2010). ISBN: 978-988-19932-4-3.

About the Author

Lawrence is poet, musician, writer and mathematician. He has written two published books, the epic poem *Astra and Sebastian* (a finalist for the Proverse Prize, 2010) and a biography of Cornish ceramicists Troika, *Troika 1963-83.*

Summary of the Book by the Author

Astra and Sebastian can be seen as an epic tale of adventure and love but for me it is more personal than that. Certain events in my life, the early death of my father, my diagnosis and subsequent cure from cancer, led me to question ideas of permanence and how we can connect to the vast universe flying around us. I found myself becoming enamoured with ideas from psychoanalysis, history, philosophy and mythology.

The poem is a response to how we find ourselves in a transient world and yet can retain moments of everlasting sadness or bliss. Through Astra and Sebastian's journey I wanted to shed some light onto those aspects of our lives which are at once too big to comprehend or are so small they can vanish without us ever having been fully aware of their importance.

After such an epic adventure, like Astra and Sebastian, I was suddenly able to appreciate the simple pleasure of being at home watching the stars pass overhead with those I love. ~~~

THE DAY THEY CAME by Gérard Louis Breissan. HK & UK, March 2012. Pbk. 160pp. ISBN-13: 978-988-19934-6-5

About the Author

Gerard Louis Breissan is a native of Aix en Provence, South of

France, and a Canadian citizen. Since 2005 he has been living in China, where he is the Head of the Hospitality and Tourism department at Jilin University Lambton College in Changchun. He has always had a passion for writing.

Summary of the Book by the Author
The Day They Came is the exhilarating and gripping semi-fictional story of a French teenager in the South of France who witnesses an UFO landing while at a summer camp near his hometown. He meets an alien named Eudoxus who becomes his mentor and guardian angel. Eudoxus saves the young man's life on many occasions. Then there is Etienne the fisherman who narrates his terrifying ordeal during a freak storm off Le Grau du Roi in the French Camargue, where six men perish at sea. The readers then travel to the African Congo where our author is now a mercenary operating with the French Special Forces who encounter the ruthless Simba warriors and a mysterious ageless Jesuite missionary named father Lapineau. Year after year Eudoxus never stops watching over the young man and keeps him alive.

In this novel the author exhibits courage, resilience and a deep faith to remain true to himself and follow the right path in life.

INSTANT MESSAGES, by Laura Solomon. HK & UK, 2010. Pbk. 168pp. Joint-Winner of the Proverse Prize (2009). ISBN-13: 978-988-19320-2-0.

About the Author
Laura Solomon was bought up in New Zealand and has worked in Australia, London and Norway. She began writing fiction at the age of fourteen and published her first novel at twenty-one.

Summary of the Book by the Author
Instant Messages is a novella aimed at teenage readers but also for adults who are interested in teenage life. Set in contemporary London, the novel is narrated by Olivia Best, a fifteen year old computer nerd who, along with her stuffed toy Green Frog, sets about navigating her way through life in the twenty-first century. Her mother, an accountant, has left her husband and twin daughters to live with her lesbian lover. Her father, Alan Best, is a wannabe novelist whose work is frequently

rejected by agents and publishers. Olivia's troubled twin sister is Melanie, a self-harmer who regularly smokes and drinks herself into a state of unconsciousness. Olivia is frequently bullied by a gang of boys from a neighbouring estate. The novel addresses the over-looked problem of childhood and teenage bullying.

WANNABE BACKPACKERS: THE LATIN AMERICAN & KENYAN JOURNEY OF FIVE SPOILED TEENAGERS by Gerald Yeung. HK & UK, 2009. Pbk. 164pp. inc. several b/w pix. ISBN: 978-988-17724-2-8.

About the Author

Gerald Yeung is a finalist in the San Francisco Writing Contest 2013 (non-fiction). He spoke at the writers' panel in the 2012 Hong Kong Book Fair and his work has appeared on *Youth.gov.hk*. *Wannabe Backpackers* (Proverse, 2009) is his first book.

Summary of the Book by the Author

On the year they turn twenty, Gerald and his four childhood friends decide to take the world by storm. The five delicate princesses embark on a round-the-world backpacking journey and, in typical Hong Kong boy fashion, immediately want to go home. *Wannabe Backpackers: The Latin American and Kenyan Journey of Five Spoiled Teenagers* chronicles this epic misadventure, defined by their relentless pursuit of urban comfort in the remotest frontiers of the world. From sipping the legendary Machu Picchu cocktail to gawking at Masai Mara's infamous toilet, from surviving embarrassing rejections to fending off all-too-eager suitors, and from abandoning each other on foreign soil to laughing together through good times and bad, they come home with a newfound appreciation for friendship, happiness, life. To this day, they remain the most incompetent backpackers known to man.~~~